JUST ONE KISS

J. SAMAN

Fall in love with
just one kiss!
♡
J. Saman

Chapter One

LONDON

"Dad, just stop. It can't be helped," I groan, leaning back in the seat of my two-door Boxster, heading up I-91 North through Vermont on the way to my parents' winter home through what appears to be the beginnings of a storm. "The Weather Channel mentioned some snow. Like three-to-six inches max. I'm sure it's going to be fine."

"When was the last time you checked that?"

I have to think about this for a second. It's been a long couple of days. "I don't know. Friday?"

"It's Monday, London," he not so kindly points out, his tone growing shrill and agitated. "Monday. Weather changes in this part of the country on a daily basis. We're supposed to get eighteen-to-twenty-four inches at a *minimum,* and it's expected to come down fast and hard with the added bonus of some ice mixing in. Hence why your mother and I have both been calling you non-stop for the last two days. The last two days that you've been ignoring us."

I bluster out a frustrated breath. "I was on deadline."

"I know. You told us that on Friday. At the exact same time we told you that you can work from anywhere."

I roll my eyes like the petulant child he's making me feel like. "Stop it with that. I can't write in a house full of people screaming and watching old movies and shouting at me about decorating the tree or which color of tinsel works best."

"Or making out like two horny teenagers," I hear my sister grouse in the background, the ick in her voice unmistakable and loud, since my father always has to have me on speakerphone. Why? Who the fuck knows! That's just how he rolls.

"Your mother and I have not been making out like two horny teenagers."

"Liar," she coughs. "They're worse than me and Maverick." Maverick is my eldest sister, Charleston's—or Charlie as we call her—fiancé. That's obviously not his real name, but since my sister's favorite movie is *Meet The Parents* (Not *Top Gun*, as you would think) everyone calls him Maverick since she's his Iceman. I don't question the logic behind it, since technically it was Goose to his Maverick and Goose dies, but it's really not worth the effort.

"You wanna talk about horny people going at it all the time, go pop in on Savannah and Royce. They've been like bunnies in heat since she got pregnant." That's my mother chiming in, and I can't help but growl into the phone.

"How do you think they got pregnant in the first place?" Charlie cackles.

"You know what?" I interject, my nose scrunched up. "Maybe I'll turn back around. You're right, the weather is getting bad."

Being the only single in a house full of over-love and over-sharing can get to be a bit much.

Especially this time of year.

My mother laughs, knowing I'm kidding. As much as I know my family is crazy, I love them to pieces and then a bunch more. And it's Christmas. The universal time to be with family, crazy or otherwise.

At least that's how we do it.

No matter what's going on in our lives, we stop and get together as a family. It's tradition. Evidently I'm a little late to the party.

"If you had tried to write from here, you'd already be *here*, safe and sound," my father cuts in, hating my mother's over-sharing as much as I do. "But instead you're driving into an area with blizzard warnings in a car that does not have front-wheel drive, let alone all-wheel drive. You could have stopped at the house and picked up one of the SUVs, London. I swear, sometimes you just love screwing with my sanity and blood pressure." He sighs and I fall silent. "Where are you?" he asks, his tone softening. "Maybe you *should* just turn back or find a place to stay that's safe. As much as I need you here to help me balance out your sisters and your mother, I'm worried about you driving in this."

I glance over at my navigation screen and then quickly back to the road. The snow is falling so thickly, I can hardly see the road ahead of me that is so terribly plowed, it's ridiculous. This is ski country after all, is it not? Isn't plowing snow what these people live for up here?

"It looks like I'm close to I-89." I think. It's nearly impossible to tell, even on the navigation screen because every few seconds, it cycles like it's lost. Not all that reassuring.

My dad starts cursing into the phone. "In this weather, that will take you a minimum of two to three hours. Find a motel, London. I don't like you driving in this."

"Dad, the day after tomorrow is Christmas Eve. The day after that Christmas. I just want to get there and be with all of you for the holiday. Who knows how long this storm could go on for?"

"That's why we told you to come up three days ago!"

"Blood pressure," I remind him. "And now is not the time for the I-told-you-so speech."

"London, for the sake *of* my blood pressure and your mother's, please. I'll send Fletcher down to fetch you with an all-wheel drive truck, but I hate you driving in that Porsche."

I look to my left and right out my foggy windows, but there is nothing but evergreens and snow. No towns. No signs. Not even a roadside gas station.

I puff out a resigned sigh. "Okay, I'll find something," I tell him, hoping this weather abates a bit so I can just push on and make it up to the house.

"Call or text when you're somewhere safe. We love you."

"Love you too, Dad." I disconnect the call, wiping with my hand against my windshield that is fogging up despite the defroster I have going and the heat I have blasting.

I left New York at eight this morning and the snow started once I hit the Connecticut/Massachusetts border. It's now noon, which means I've been driving in this mess forever, epically slowed down to practically a crawl since the roads are slick and visibility is shit. There are no other cars on the road, and this is what you'd call a major highway. No holiday traffic or ski warriors who are not deterred by the treacherous white stuff.

It makes no sense to me unless they were smart enough to leave early and beat the storm. Obviously, I need to check my weather app more often or (shudder) listen to my parents more than I do.

Instead, I am alone in a car that is not meant for this, going about twenty-five miles per hour and hoping—hell praying—that I don't miss the exit for I-89 that will lead me up toward Burlington and my parents' house on Lake Champlain, hovering a solid ten miles from the Canadian border.

This wouldn't have been so bad if I could have snaked my way up through New York and then over into Vermont, but no, the highway north of the city showed a massive accident this morning and my GPS rerouted me. My stomach growls loudly, choosing this moment to remind me that I haven't had anything to eat all day since I woke up late and had to run out the door, slurping down a to-go coffee from the deli on the corner by my apartment.

"Don't start," I snap at my empty belly. "I can't feed you. We have to make it through this shit first."

Turning up the music humming through my speakers, I lean forward, singing aloud to a song I know by heart. It helps to settle my slightly frazzled nerves and I push forward, scanning every snow-covered sign for the one I need. But as the miles stretch and the road grows more and more empty, my heart rate begins to spike with panic.

Did I miss it? Did I miss the exit?

Just as those thoughts hit me hard, my GPS starts in with 're-calculating route' in that annoying, nasal voice it has. I glance over to the map, but it's like my car is driving out into the middle of nowhere and not on a highway. The gray circle in the center of it just keeps spinning and spinning, and this is the moment that I go from a seven on the panic scale to twenty-eight.

"Balls," I curse. "You're supposed to run on a freaking satellite," I yell at the screen.

I slow down further, glancing out my window first and then the passenger one. But it's all the same, and I have no idea where I am. In a moment of desperation, I hit the button on my steering wheel to bring up my phone so I can call my father back, but now that's not even working. All the names and numbers are gray.

What the hell is going on?!

Picking up my phone from my center console, I unlock it with my face only to find that I have no service. As in none. Zero. Not even 3G.

"Dammit!" I scream at the top of my lungs, slamming my fist into the button to shut off the music that is happily chirping from my speakers. "Shut up!" I yell at it, running a frazzled hand through my hair and trying to rein myself in. Panicking like this will get me nowhere. I need to think. I need to calm the hell down.

Sucking in a deep, meant to be fortifying breath, I straighten my spine and steel my nerves and resolve.

I catch a sign that says something about a glass warehouse, a motel, a gas station, and *yes*. "That's what I'm talking about!"

But in my stupid enthusiasm, I press a little too hard on the gas pedal, and as if my car is chastising me the way my father would, the front tires start to slip and sway, skidding on the packed snow and ice that coats the road.

"No," I bellow, my voice skipping up a notch to a startled screech as the back tires start to get in on the action, overcompensating for the front. "Stop that. Don't do this. Please, I swear, I'll ease into whatever motel I find if you just stop doing that." My hands grip the steering wheel tighter, twisting it to the right and then the left frantically, trying to realign the suddenly out-of-control vehicle.

Oh my god, this cannot be happening.

My foot hits the brake and the wheel shimmies, the tires making a horrific grating noise. I press on the gas once more, but instead of correcting the problem as I anticipated, the car starts to spin, doing a full 360. I slam back on the brakes but to no avail.

We're not stopping.

We're not even slowing down.

If anything, the car is moving faster. Terrifyingly so. My heart is racing out of my chest, blood thrumming through my ears at a deafening decibel.

My hands are flying this way and that, but now the car is gaining speed, heading straight for… "Ahhhh!" I scream, my eyes wide and unblinking, my hands white-knuckling the wheel as I barrel toward a row of trees on the side of the highway without any way to stop.

My eyes close just at the moment of impact, my body tense and coiled as the front driver's side hits the tree with a sickening *crunch*.

The impact throws me, my head smashing into the window, and then my body lurches, slamming against the steering wheel. No airbags. I have no idea why they didn't deploy in a seventy-thousand-dollar car, but that's a serious problem as my head explodes with blinding pain.

Warm stickiness dribbles down my face as the car shifts and moves a little more before stopping completely, wedged against and under the tree.

I fall back into my seat, panting for my life and searching around the car. I sit here for a stunned, silent moment, mentally assessing everything. I have no idea if anything else is injured other than my forehead. I move my toes in my Uggs then my fingers.

"Jesus Christ. I can't believe I just crashed," I whisper.

Outside, I see nothing but white. Trees and an endless fucking sea of white.

I glance down at my lap and then over to the console, but I can't find my phone. A splatter of blood drips from my face onto my jeans.

Blood.

Oh my god. My stomach immediately rolls as my vision sways. I take a few deep breaths, forcing myself not to think about that.

About the red, wet, sticky stuff that's now everywhere. I touch it with my fingers and that's just the wrong thing for me to do because it makes the dizziness worse. But holy bejesus, it really *is* everywhere. I scramble for my purse that fell into the well on the passenger side, searching for something, anything that will help wipe the blood off my face and body.

I have to get rid of it.

Dizziness consumes me as I move. A fresh wave of nausea hits me hard, cold sweat coating my skin like bad makeup. I close my eyes, fighting the black prickly dots around the edges of my vision before I reopen them, find my purse, and pull out my pack of tissues.

I wad up a ball in my hand and press the paper into the cut on my forehead. A whimper passes my lips at the sharp, shooting pain that accompanies that, but I soldier on, determined to find my phone and get the hell out of here.

My cell is on the other side of the passenger seat, but the second I pick it up, I know it's useless. I had no service before the crash and looking at the screen now, I see it's no different.

Fucking hell. What am I going to do now?

Chapter Two

MILES

"Knew he was a killer first time that I saw him..." Taylor Swift, unfortunately, sings through my speakers as Betsy howls appreciatively, snuggling into my side and bumping my shoulder with her nose.

"Don't cuddle up to me," I warn her. "We really need to have a serious discussion about your taste in music. It's insanely emasculating that I allow my dog to dictate the music choice in my own truck. If anyone ever saw this, I'd never hear the end of it."

Not that anyone is ever in my truck besides me or Betsy, but still. It wouldn't be good. And really any excuse to get rid of this once and for all, I'll take.

Betsy is undeterred by my threats. She knows they're baseless.

She nudges me again, barks, and I sigh, pressing a button on my steering wheel to turn up the angsty chick music. When I rescued her from the shelter last month, this is what came with her. Taylor Swift. "It's the only thing that soothes her," the girl told me with a gleam in her eye as she tried, and failed, to hide her smile.

So here we are. Driving along the snow-covered highway, headed home with a truck full of groceries that will last us well through the new year, listening to Taylor belt out song after song. Some pop. Some country.

All giving me a headache.

I have the plow on the front of my truck up, but as the snow is really coming down, I'm starting to debate lowering it to clear some of the highway. If not just for me, but other motorists coming this way as it doesn't seem like the state has started plowing yet.

This storm hit us quickly and a bit unexpectedly.

What was supposed to be a small dusting, just a few inches, has turned into a nice old nor'easter, complete with ice and wind and buckets of heavy snow. Personally, I love it when it gets like this. I hunker down in my shop and ignore the outside world. No tourists I have to make nice with coming through. Just me and my work.

Well, and now Betsy.

But uninterrupted peace and quiet.

Exactly the way I like to spend the holidays.

Just as I decelerate and lower the plow to tackle some of the heavy wet stuff, Betsy starts barking. Loud and urgently. She shuffles across her seat, pressing her snout against the foggy glass, scratching at the door.

"What's up, girl? I can't let you out here. The snow is coming down too hard. We'll be home in fifteen minutes. You can hold it until then."

But she's not giving up, growing more demanding by the second, and that's when I catch it—the flash of glowing red amidst the white about fifty yards off into the woods.

Shit. A car must have lost control and crashed.

"Alright, girl. I see it. Calm down." I pat Betsy's back, slowing down and plowing my way over to the side of the highway. I don't dare take the truck into the bank. Though it could probably handle it, I'd rather not risk getting stuck myself. I stop, placing the truck in park and narrowing my eyes through the windshield, trying to get a better look at what I'm facing.

The tiny sporty convertible looks like it hit a tree, but I can't see anyone. They're probably still in the car instead of trying to brave the elements. I'm tempted to call the police, but I need to know the situation of the driver or other passengers before I do that.

If it's just the car that's stuck and no one is hurt, I can call Earl, who might be able to drag it out of here before things get any worse.

But if they're hurt, that's a different story.

The nearest hospital from here is a solid thirty miles away and in this weather, that might as well be a hundred.

"You stay here," I tell Betsy, zipping up my coat and throwing my hood over my beany because it's cold as hell out. I hit the button for my hazard lights and open the door against the blustering icy wind and snow that assault me instantly. I jump down, right into over a foot of snow, some of it from the storm we had last week and shut the door behind me.

Tucking myself in, I jog in my boots as quickly as I can manage over toward the car that is still running. The front fender is crushed up against the tree, but otherwise it seems okay. I reach the driver's side door, spotting a dark form inside pressed against the seat. I can't make out much as the windows are entirely fogged over with condensation, so I knock.

"Hey," I call out, trying not to scare them. "You okay in there?"

"Yes. I think so," a female voice returns, but she makes no move to open the door. I nearly roll my eyes.

"Do you need some help?"

"I…"

"Did you call the police?"

No reply.

"Ma'am, are you alone in the car? Are you hurt?"

"I, um. Yeah, I'm alone." I hear her curse something out. "I have no cell service. No cell service," she repeats. "How is that possible? My phone works everywhere in the city."

Great. One of these people.

"Maybe it's time I update my carrier? What do you think?"

I think, more like I'm hoping, she's just in shock or scared and not actually asking my opinion on her cell phone carrier.

"Can you open the door for me?" I would try it myself, but

that's not a good idea with a lone female who appears to be slightly dazed.

I hear the door click open and the cabin light inside the car flips on. She's still buckled in and no airbag deployed, which means it hopefully wasn't much of an impact. But then she turns to look up at me and her entire face is covered with smeared blood, oozing from a laceration on her hairline.

It doesn't look terrible, scalp injuries bleed like a bastard, but she definitely needs medical attention. "Are you hurt anywhere else? Your neck or back?"

She shakes her head.

"No. Just my forehead. The cold air feels good. I should have rolled down the window when I started to feel faint. Bear Grylls would be so disappointed in my survival skills."

My eyebrows hit my hairline. "Huh?"

"Never mind." She waves me away.

"Can you get out of the car? You're bleeding and you need help."

She grunts, searching around at her lap. "Please don't mention the blood. I'm barely hanging on with that. I ran out of tissues and it's just… yeah, I hate blood. It totally freaks me out." She lets out a bitter, humorless laugh. "For a girl who grew up in New England, you'd think I would be better prepared, but no. I drove up here in my car instead of renting one or stopping to get one of my father's. Speaking of which, he's going to kill me. I decided I couldn't meet my deadline with my family breathing down my neck, so I stayed in the city until the last minute. Now look at me. I'm a mess. And there's blood. So much blood."

"How hard did you hit your head?"

She makes some kind of scoffing, snorting sound in the back of her throat. "I'm going to take that as a serious question and not a dig that's questioning my sanity in this moment because that would be insanely rude and ill-timed. But to answer your question, I'm honestly not sure. Should there be this much blood?"

"How about you start with unbuckling your seat belt, okay? The snow is coming down pretty hard and I'd like to get you out of here."

She presses the button on her car, shutting it off and stuffing her phone back into her purse. She unbuckles her seat belt, her midnight hair sticking to the side of her face. Touching her forehead, she winces at the blood coating her fingers. What I can see of her face turns white as a sheet.

"I really am a mess." She pants out a few choppy breaths, her body swaying slightly. "My father is not going to be happy with me. Did I already say that? Do you have any idea how aggravating it is to be told, I told you so, from your father who is always right?"

"No," I tell her in all seriousness, the familiar pinch accompanying the word whenever I think about my father. "Come on." I hold out my hand to her and she slides her small, warm hand into mine. A weird spark of static electricity hits my skin, but I quickly shake it off as I pull her up gently, letting her do most of the work so I can assess the extent of her injuries.

"My knee hurts," she says just as she buckles, my arms coming out reflexively to catch her. "Yikes. I'm really in trouble, aren't I?" She tilts her chin up, her bloody face meeting mine until she opens her eyes and I find myself staring helplessly into a field of lavender, startling and unexpected, I've only seen this color once before.

She blinks a few times, though I can't seem to manage the action. Hell, I can't even breathe. The space in my chest that was previously little more than a dead lump is suddenly sprinting so hard it sounds like a freight train running through my ears.

"I know your face," she whispers, her voice drifting. Tilting her head in my arms, she leans farther into me on a sleepy breath. She manages a half-smile, but she's slipping fast. "Though I don't remember the beard the last time I saw it," she murmurs, her eyes closing and her body growing limp in my arms. I catch her as she tries to fall through my hands, adjusting her until I'm lifting her up, tucking her protectively into my chest.

For a second, I stare down at the unconscious woman in my arms, unable to move from the sideswipe of shock that's radiating through me.

It seems impossible that it's her, though I don't know why.

Maybe it's just that seeing her again feels like someone kicked me in the gut before shoving my head under water.

I brush some of her matted hair from her face, just so I know. Just so I can confirm what every other piece of me is already acutely aware of. Snow falls on her, melting as it hits her warm, pale face, sticky with blood. She shudders in my arms, her eyes scrunching as if she's in pain.

"It's okay. I've got you."

Without another sound, I turn on my heels and march her back to my truck, trudging through freezing cold and heavy snow that's almost already covered my tracks though it's been no more than ten minutes. I force myself not to think. Not to go back in time.

I just act on instinct.

Shuffling her small body in my arms, I open the door to my warm car, Betsy sitting on the seat with large, brown, curious eyes.

"In the back, girl. We've got company."

Without argument, Betsy does as she's told. Goddamn Taylor Swift is still having a laugh at me as I slide… London Canterbury onto the passenger seat of my truck. I shift her over, mindful of her injuries, and reach across, buckling her in.

I don't take a deep breath.

I refuse to inhale her sweet fragrance that hits me square in the chest, so familiar and so exotic and so…

I clear my throat, staring at her face.

She really is a mess and I pop open the glove box, taking out some wipes I have and cleaning up her face a bit. I don't even know why I'm bothering right now. Hell, I'm still standing in the snow with the fucking door open.

But once she's cleaned up, I put the wipes away and watch her for a very long second as visions of her float helplessly through my mind. "Right, then. Only one thing to do." I slam the door shut, trudge back to her car, gather her stuff from the inside of her car and pop the trunk. I find the suitcases I assumed I would and grab them, carrying them both back to my truck.

I hop in, tossing both of the designer bags onto the seat beside

Betsy and slam my door shut, shivering against the cold and snow that has saturated my jeans and down into my socks inside my boots.

I chance one more glimpse at a passed-out London and then put the truck in drive, the plow in the front ready to guide our way. I dial up Earl and tell him where he can find her Porsche, asking him to tow it over to my place.

I glance down at London one last time, making sure she's buckled in and as comfortable as she can be. Like a star in my hand, I already feel the burn of this woman on my skin. I clear the thoughts away and pull out from the side of the road, heading home.

It seems Betsy and I have an unexpected guest.

Chapter Three

LONDON

Rolling over onto my side in the warm, soft bed, I smile to myself, grateful that I'm no longer sleeping and that horrible nightmare is over. God, it felt so real. I take in a deep breath and freeze instantly. The smell. Cologne or aftershave, I can't tell which, but it's rugged and masculine and sexy. Earthy almost, like musk and snow and sandalwood and goddamn pine trees.

Not a dream.

Miles Ford.

Is this what he smells like?

Blinking open my eyes, the first thing I see is a raging fire in a huge stone fireplace. The second is the large chocolate lab sitting on a plush white rug directly in front of the fire, staring directly at me. I blink some more, my hand reaching up to gingerly touch the cut on my forehead, only to find it covered with a bandage.

I shift as quietly as I can against the pillow my head is resting on and peek down at myself. I'm on a couch, not a bed, covered in a heavy white down comforter, still wearing the clothes I left New York in.

How long have I been unconscious for?

Freaking blood. That's the third time I've passed out from the sight of it.

My parents and sisters must be going out of their minds.

I shift some more, surreptitiously glancing around and taking in my surroundings. It's a large cabin-style home without the horrendous stuffed animal head decorative accents. Actually, this place has a lot of dark woods, brown leather, and white linen with soft throw pillows in navy blue and gray. The art on the walls is out of this world gorgeous.

The house is pretty and a bit unexpected, if I'm being honest.

It's Restoration Hardware meets Vermont in a really cool way.

The dog whimpers in my direction, wagging its tail excitedly, and I sit up slowly, not sure what to make of the fact that I'm likely in Miles's home. Sliding my legs along the fabric sofa, I wince as I move my knee and then practically yelp out in pain as I try to bend it. I don't even remember hitting it, but then again, I was a bit distracted with the car crash and the blood pouring down my face.

The dog gets up, padding directly over to me and panting right in my face. "You're sweet, but your dog breath is not." It makes some kind of noise and sets its face down on my lap. "Sorry. That was rude. We just met and I didn't mean to hurt your feelings." I absently run my fingers through its thick, soft fur. "Where is your owner?" I ask.

"I'm here," a smooth, whisky baritone announces behind me and I catch the sound of bare feet against hardwood floors headed in my direction. For a moment, nerves get the best of me, my heart jumping up into my chest while my belly does some kind of weird Macarena-esque dance.

Miles Ford.

I haven't seen him in what? Eight years?

Not since graduation night. Not since—

"How are you feeling?" he asks, interrupting my thoughts, that deep russet voice of his bathed in concern. Did he sound like this when we were teenagers? Likely not.

Tamping down the rush of nerves, I look up. And up. And eventually find his intense navy blue eyes wrapped in thick dark frames.

He has a beard, the one I think I embarrassingly mentioned to him earlier, and he's much taller and broader than the boy from my memories. Definitely hotter too, with his warm brown hair in wild disarray and face that even through the well-trimmed beard, boasts a strong chiseled jaw. He's wearing a thermal gray shirt that hugs his muscular arms and chest like they're lovers who hate to be separated.

Unfortunately, that's where my perusal ends as he's staring expectantly at me, head now tilting to the side and eyes that look as though they're questioning the extent of my head injury. Right. Because he asked me a question and I've remained silent while ogling him like a drooling buffoon.

Super classy, London. Way to slay it, girl.

"I'm fine," I finally manage, though I'm not entirely sure that's true. "Considering I was in a car accident, stuck in the snow, smashed my head, and somehow hurt my knee." I shut my mouth, wondering where the fuck my filter went.

"I cleaned and bandaged your head. It's a good gash, but it doesn't need stitches. It had pretty much stopped bleeding by the time I got you here. I couldn't check your knee without removing your jeans, and I figured I'd leave that honor to you so you or your boyfriend wouldn't have to kick my ass later." He smirks, the sight of it doing funny things to my insides.

I blink at him. *Is he fishing?* "And I appreciate that," I tease back. "Since I have no boyfriend at the present, it would only be me kicking your ass and I'm not sure my knee is up to the challenge at the moment."

He has no noticeable reaction, so maybe I was wrong about the fishing thing.

I clear my throat. "Where am I?"

"My place," he says in a tone that would suggest that was obvious. I guess it is and maybe that was a stupid question, but it's not exactly what I was asking.

The question was meant to be, "Why am I here?"

He runs a hand through his hair, and I wonder if he's been doing that a lot given the state of it. "Because you passed out in my arms after I found you in your car, stuck and bleeding. It's a blizzard outside, and the nearest hospital might as well be in Canada for how accessible it is in this weather. Honestly, I didn't know where else to take you. Bringing you here just seemed like the easy call to make." He shrugs, his tone a bit defensive.

I nod, feeling bad. I didn't mean for it to come out accusingly. "Thank you for saving me. Who knows what would have happened to me if you hadn't shown up, Miles." Then I smile, shaking my head and laughing lightly under my breath. "Wow, it really is you. For a minute or two, I thought I imagined you. It's been such a long time—"

"You're welcome, London," he quickly interjects in a tone I don't quite understand. It's not angry, but there is a distinct edge to it and my smile slips instantly into a frown.

Dragging my gaze away from him, I search for my purse. I need to call my parents. Find my car. Get out of his hair, because that's clearly what he wants. I've obviously imposed upon him enough.

I ignore the sour resin that leaves in my mouth and ask, "Did you happen to grab my purse? I'll just make a couple of calls and be out of your hair in a jiffy."

"Your phone likely doesn't have service here if it didn't where I found you on the highway, but you're welcome to use mine."

I sag a little at that. At the fact that my phone still doesn't have service. It's a disconcerting feeling. Almost like being stranded. Oh wait, I am stranded.

I want to offer something up to him. An apology maybe. He rescued me and I passed out in his arms and now I'm in his home, taking up his time and space.

But it's Miles. Miles Ford. I seriously still cannot wrap my head around that. It's cool and weird and a bit exciting, if I'm being honest.

The fact that he's a dish of ice cream only makes this crazier.

"London," he starts, his tone softening, and I instantly look back up, wanting to catalog more of him if only for comparison to my memories. Okay, that's a half-lie. He's really great to look at, and let's be frank here, it's been a damn long time since just the sight of a guy got me hot under the collar—or panties as the case may be. "You don't have to feel like you need to leave. You're hurt and it's late—already dark. Not to mention the weather outside. I think it's safe to say, you're stuck here with me for a bit."

Oh right. The blizzard.

I nearly forgot all about that.

I was too distracted by his sharp jawline and adorable nerdy glasses that make his blues look even bigger and brighter. Who knew such a thing was possible?

My gaze falls, staring at my hands and I notice the blood covering my shirt. My head swims, but I push it back. "Dammit," I whisper. "Miles, I'm so unbelievably sorry. I didn't mean to put you out like this. This is so much more than you bargained for when you stopped to help a stranded motorist. I bet from now on, you'll think twice before you do such a noble and heroic act."

He moves closer, demanding my attention. When I glance back up, he's grinning with that adorable smile I remember from once upon a time. Dimples and all, even through the beard. God, those dimples always killed me.

"You didn't put me out, London. Nothing to be sorry about. I'm just glad you're okay."

I swallow thickly at that. I very nearly was not. He watches me for a moment, his eyes dancing about my face the way mine are with him. Something inside of me begins to speed up. My heart goes into a flutter as my stomach dips with a sensation resembling anticipation.

But for what, I'm not entirely sure.

It's the way he's looking at me.

His smile is long gone, but it's like there is something hidden behind his reformed, stoic mask. Silence collapses in on us, thick and heavy like the blanket still covering my lower half. I wonder if he's thinking about the last time we saw each other.

About the bonfire.

I wonder if he's remembering the art class I took when art was never my thing. I wonder if he's remembering the hour and a half we had to spend together in the library every day because we both had a creative writing independent study and that's where we were instructed to go to work on our projects. He barely ever spoke to me there, but I'd catch him looking at me more than I wouldn't.

I doubt he has any idea as to how that daily library session forever changed the fabric of my life. Made me who I am. Created the world I now reside in.

I've thought about Miles Ford over the years. In many ways. The questions lingered if for no other reason than the mystery behind him.

He disappeared.

Graduated. Came to the party that night. Then gone. Poof.

I know because I went looking for him after that night.

After what happened between us.

His eyes slip down to my lips, holding on for a long beat before they slide effortlessly down the rest of me as I sit here like a wounded doll on his sofa with his dog's head on my lap, my fingers still absently brushing at its fur. Finally, he clears his throat and whatever spell we're momentarily lost in is gone.

"I brought your suitcases from your car and asked a buddy of mine to have it towed here. It's in my garage already. Feel free to take a shower or change or whatever you need. There's a guest room at the top of the stairs at the end of the hall. I changed the linens and it has its own bathroom." He points to the stairs behind him. "The landline works the best when it's snowing like this. There is one in that room, I think."

I stare, stunned, only able to jerk out a small nod. He changed the sheets. Brought up my suitcases. Had my car towed here. He stopped to help when he saw my car and bandaged up my wound— Superhero *Miles to the rescue.*

"Thank you, Captain America. I know I'm saying thank you a lot, but I'm not even sure how else to express my gratitude."

He belts out a startled laugh. "Captain America?"

I shrug. "Though I wish I were as fierce as the Black Widow in this moment, I think it's safe to say you saved my damsel in distress from her sticky situation. And" —I tilt my head, smirking before I can stop the playful gesture— "you have blue eyes and brown hair. Same as him."

"I thought he was blond?"

I grin. "Chris Evans? Nope."

"You'd look weird with red hair," he comments, almost as if he's talking to himself. "Red hair and violet eyes?" He shakes his head, rubbing a hand at his jaw and I know it's to hide his grin. I think he might even be blushing, and damn, he's so cute. Such a rugged, burly man's man, but still so nerdy in his glasses and dimples and smiles.

"How long is this storm supposed to last?" I ask, changing the subject and going back to safe, fact-based territory. The idea of staying here alone with Miles in his house doing things to me it shouldn't.

"Not sure. A couple of days at the most. I have a generator, so even if we lose power, it won't be an issue."

A couple of days? Losing power?

I hadn't even considered that. That the storm would last that long. That we could lose power. That I would be stuck here with the sexy mountain man who doesn't seem all that jazzed about having me for a houseguest.

"Where were you headed?"

"Up near the Canadian border to Lake Champlain. My parents have a place there. Is there any way—"

"No. Not when it's coming down like this. That's still a ways from here, over an hour in good weather."

"It's almost Christmas," I mumble dejectedly.

"I suppose it is. With any luck, the storm will clear out faster than expected and you can get back to whoever and wherever you were headed for the holidays."

"What about you and your holiday? I didn't mean…" I trail off, unsure how to finish that. I nearly say ruined your Christmas, but there isn't a stitch of anything remotely Christmas-y or holiday-ish here. You'd never know that the day after tomorrow is Christmas Eve.

He stares me down another long minute, his eyes flickering

about my face before finally looking away, staring off into his kitchen, his posture stiff and his expression cast from stone.

"Dinner is almost ready. You must be hungry." And it's only now that I catch the scent of something heavenly cooking. Something that smells like stew and my stomach growls accordingly. He must hear it because I catch a small grin bouncing up the corner of his lips. "Why don't you go get cleaned up. Do you need any help up the stairs?"

Good question, but considering the situation I find myself in, there is no way I'm going to ask him for anything else. I feel bad enough as it is.

"No. I can manage." I stand up slowly, moving the blanket back to the couch. My knee hurts like a mother-effer, but I suck it up and deal.

He nods, heading off for the kitchen like just being in the same general proximity as me is painful. I frown again, looking over at his dog and shrugging. It nudges me in the leg as if to say, well, get a move on then.

Sucking in a rush of air, I walk, doing my best not to limp or cry, over to the stairs, grasping the thick wood railing and taking them one at a time.

I chance a glance over my shoulder, but I don't see Miles. He's back in the kitchen and hidden behind the wall from my view. Good.

After an eternity, I make it upstairs, but before I can find the room he mentioned, I hear him call out my name. I freeze, staring down at him over the balcony that overlooks the great room beneath, waiting patiently while he works through whatever it is that had him saying my name.

He blows out a harsh breath and says, "I never thought I'd see you again."

Me either, I think.

"I'm glad you're okay," he says again. "You scared me when you passed out."

I stare at him and wonder what's happened to him in the last eight years. Miles was always quiet. A lot cute and a bit nerdy. Sort of sad, now that I think about it. But sweet. He never had this… edge to him.

"I put some stuff to bandage your knee in there along with a few different types of pain medicines in case you need them."

God. This man.

Without waiting on my reply, he stalks off, back to the kitchen and I stare after him, something in my chest I'm not familiar with twinging. "Thank you, Miles," I whisper. This could be a very long couple of days.

Chapter Four

LONDON

Entering the guest room, I look around. It's big. Like the rest of the house, I'm starting to realize. It has a king-size bed, two nightstands, a dresser, and a bay window that overlooks the entire back yard. I go there first, hobbling like an old woman as I go.

I whistle through my teeth, not only at the snow falling in thick blankets of white, but at what I can make out of the large sprawling property. My suitcases are both set up on the cushioned bench at the foot of the bed and my purse and computer bag are sitting on a fabric chair in the corner.

I shake my head, still unable to get all this in, and open my suitcase, pulling out some comfy, but cute pajamas. I would dress up a little if I wouldn't look foolish doing it, but my knee is seriously miserable, and I decide comfort over fashion is the way to go.

It's not like Miles will care or notice anyway.

I strip down, hobbling my broken ass into the bathroom, only to gasp. A double marble vanity, antique white tile floor, large walk-in glass shower with subway tile, and a huge clawfoot tub. "Miles Ford, you are certainly unexpected."

The bathroom is gorgeous.

But it's the array of items on the counter that has me saying that about him.

There are three bottles of pills, Tylenol, Advil, and a prescription bottle of something stronger. There are bandages, gauze, tape, scissors, cleaning solutions, and ointments. The shower is loaded with what looks like brand-new shampoos, conditioners, and body washes and I wonder how many guests he's had over because the man certainly knows what he's doing.

From what I can tell, he lives here alone with his dog.

I didn't hear or see anyone else, and he certainly didn't mention anyone.

There were no personal pictures on his mantle. None on his walls either, just a lot of colorful art. "Who are you, Miles?"

I'm not sure I ever knew.

I noticed him instantly when he came to our school. All the girls did, but once they found out he was a scholarship kid, liked to keep mostly to himself, and didn't fawn all over them, they lost interest quickly.

Not me.

I had boyfriends and went to parties and led my high school life, but I always watched him. Was always curious and crushing if we're speaking the truth here.

He was a country on to himself and there was something about that that intrigued me. He had a story no one knew, and I envied that in a way. Especially since everyone and their great-grandmother knew mine.

Knew my family.

A queen bee though I never quite understood the how or the why behind it.

I couldn't hold hands with a guy in the dark without the entire school, my sisters, and my parents hearing about it.

Miles seemed above it all.

Keeping to himself by choice. Taking art classes, never going to parties or trying to befriend the popular kids. He seemed to have a freedom, a quiet confidence I was unfamiliar with.

Turning on the shower to hot, I peel off the bandage on my

head, taking in the cleaned one-inch slice. It's not bleeding anymore, as Miles said, but it's red and pretty angry looking. Glancing down, I take in my right knee. No cuts or open skin, thank god, but it's already got a nasty purple bruise on it.

"You really rocked this out, London. Super job." I sigh. I just hope I don't miss Christmas with my family.

Stepping into the shower, I wash myself up quickly, and when I step out, wrapping myself in a warmed white towel, I feel a little better.

A bit more like myself.

I dress in my PJs and brush out my long hair. I apply a little makeup because let's be real here, Miles Ford is downstairs, and then I sit on the edge of the bed and pick up the phone. My parents always made us remember three phone numbers. In the age of cell phones, where all your contacts are stored, it's easy not to know anyone's number. But right now, I'm glad my parents had the foresight to push that one into us.

I call my dad's cell phone because I don't know the house number up there off the top of my head. He picks up on the first ring, worry evident in his tone.

"Hello?"

"Hi, Dad. It's me."

"London. Jesus Henry Christ, where the hell are you? We've been going out of our fluffing minds. Your mother has called every hospital in the fucking state."

Shit. I scoot back a little, running my hands down my wet strands and feeling awful. "I'm sorry. I'm fine. I swear. I… um… had a little accident." I cringe, shutting my eyes even though he can't see me.

"A little accident? What is it?"

"Well, it's when your car crashes, but that's not important right now."

"London Amelia Canterbury, I swear I will trash your Christmas presents if you ever quote *Airplane* to me again when I'm this worried about you."

I laugh despite myself. "Sorry. It was too good to pass up and I was stalling. I lost control of the car shortly after we hung up and I crashed into a tree. The car was stuck in the snow and I hit my head and knee. I'm fine," I quickly add. "Just a bit of blood from my head."

"Did you pass out? Where are you?"

I roll my eyes because my episodes with blood are legendary. I couldn't even watch the *Twilight* movies and they were not that gory. "Someone came and found me. They got me out of the car and cleaned me up and brought me to their house to stay."

"Who? Where are you?" he repeats, growing more exasperated, though you'd think it would be the opposite. You'd think knowing I'm okay, he'd be calming down, but that's not really my father's style. He likes all his chickens home and safe in front of him.

"Dad, do you remember Miles Ford?"

"Huh? Who?"

I shake my head. "Never mind. The guy who saved me turns out is someone I went to high school with. Weird coincidence, right?"

"London. Why does it sound like you're intentionally being evasive?"

"I'm not," I protest. "I'm at his home now. In Vermont," I qualify, though I'm not sure why. That probably should be obvious, but we did grow up in southern Connecticut.

"Do I know his family? Ford?"

"No. He never hung out in my circle of friends. Anyway, he's a really nice man and he saved me as I said, cleaned up my cut and everything. I'm calling from his phone. In his guest room, not his bedroom." I cover my eyes with my hand, because seriously? I just basically announced to my father that I think Miles is hot. Nothing like that ever squeaks past my family.

And in fact, my father chuckles. "You mean to tell me there is a man alive who hasn't instantly fallen for your charms."

"Dad."

"I'm only kidding, London. I'm glad he took such good care of you and I'm relieved you know him. I'd send out the national guard to get you if I thought you were staying the night in some strange man's house. You feel safe?"

"I feel safe. I just don't know when I'm going to be able to leave with the storm and my car."

"Don't worry about the car. I'll send Fletcher with one of the large SUVs once this all subsides, but they're asking people to stay off the roads. Evidently, there have already been a lot of accidents and they need the roads clear for emergency vehicles and snow-plows. But none of that matters to me. We want you here for Christmas. In the twenty-six years, you've been on this earth, you have not missed one with us and this will not be the year that happens."

Christmas with my family is a big deal. I think I already mentioned that. My dad's parents died when he was in college on Christmas in a terrible drunk driving accident. So Christmas with his family is beyond important to him. To all of us.

The one holiday we always spend together.

I need to get there. I need to make it up to my parents' place by Christmas.

"Don't worry, Dad. I'll be there," I promise, twisting my lip between my fingers as I stare out the window into the darkness. "Hopefully for Christmas Eve, but at the very least, Christmas Day."

"Okay. I'm counting on it. I'm going to tell your mother what happened. Call us tomorrow, okay?"

"Okay."

"Love you, London."

I smile. "Love you too, Daddy."

I hang up with a heaviness in my chest. I have no idea what this night or the next few days has in store for me, but I'd be lying if I said I wasn't curious about Miles. About how all this could go. After all, we're not kids anymore.

Chapter Five

MILES

"Don't give me that look," I say to Betsy while she stares at me like I was being a cold and indifferent prick. I was sure as hell trying to be and I know it, but flirting with London is my eternal moth to flame and being anything but a dick right now with her is asking for trouble.

Betsy barks at me in that pissed off bark of hers and I groan, rolling my eyes at her.

"Will you forgive me if I put on Taylor Swift?"

She's doing that dog tilt of the head thing and I know even Taylor can't fix this.

"Fine. I'll work on it," I promise my dog, who is already smitten with London. Not that I blame her. I was struck the second I saw her on my very first day walking into our high school. It was hell for me, as I knew it would be, and then I saw her, and everything changed.

London Canterbury.

My mind wanders back in time. To that first day...

I step off the bus, hiking my worn messenger bag up on my shoulder and staring down the road to the building in the distance. You'd think I would no longer feel any nerves after attending five different schools in seven years, but this one feels different. Worse, somehow.

Maybe it's the cars driving into the lot, the cheapest one being a Lexus SUV.

Maybe it's the kids jumping out of those cars with bright smiles, pristine uniforms, and designer shoes, whereas I'm marching toward them on foot, wearing sneakers that are a size too small, a second-hand uniform, and a frown.

Whatever the reason, a creeping sense of dread fills my gut as I soldier my way to the front door of the large ivy snaked brick building. I take a step inside, glancing this way and that. It smells exactly how I expected it would. Like expensive perfume and wood polish and money.

No one can make you feel inferior unless you let them.

It's a good line, but it does little to settle my nerves as I force myself away from the door, clutching my schedule in my hand like it's the one thing I've got going for me. Maybe it is. The admission person I spoke with on the phone was excited to tell me about their art program. About all the different mediums I'll have access to at no cost since they're available to all students, scholarship or not.

I meander my way through the front of the building, coming upon something resembling an atrium with five halls branching off the center. This seems to be the place all the students congregate and for a moment, I allow myself to linger on the periphery, curious about what I'll find. I was not happy about leaving my last school. I had made a couple of friends and was settling into what felt like a normal version of a life when the rug was ripped out from under me again. The foster family I was living with out of nowhere decided to move states, leaving me to bounce back into the system.

It was a brutal reminder to keep my distance. To never grow too comfortable or form attachments because nothing good lasts. The bad stuff doesn't either, *I remind myself. It's all just the pendulum of life and in three years, I'll be able to chart my own course.*

Three years.

I can do three more years of this shit.

I start off again when something, or rather someone, catches my eye. A girl everyone is standing around, and just by the nature of curiosity, I stop without thought to try to discover what has over a dozen other students flocking to be near her.

It takes me a moment to weed through the other bodies, but finally I catch the flash of midnight colored hair piled on top of her head in a pristine ponytail.

She's gazing up at one of the guys standing beside her, a tall built guy who looks like he could play professional football. He's smiling down at her like she's the sun, but it isn't until she turns her head to talk to another person and I catch sight of her that I truly understand why.

She is the sun. She is the stars and the moon and everything exquisite about the universe. I read Romeo and Juliet last year in English, and I remember thinking how fucking stupid and ridiculous Romeo was for getting thunderstruck over a girl he'd never even spoken to before. But not now and never again will I ever think that about him.

Because holy shit. This girl. This fucking girl.

My breath, trapped somewhere in chest, wheezes pathetically past my lips.

My eyes are glued, my body humming with some strange foreign sensation that I never want to go away. It's like some kind of sweet, torturous bliss. Like a pleasure-pain.

I stare, helplessly entranced by her as she laughs and talks with her friends.

She isn't wearing heels like the other girls, but she doesn't need them. She's tall, her long legs slope up to her tartan skirt that hits just above her knee. Her white blouse is tied in a knot at her waist instead of tucked in, revealing the tiniest hint of tanned, tone flesh beneath. Her blazer is draped over her arm and I'm grateful for that because if she were wearing it, I wouldn't be able to appreciate her full, perky tits that could easily fill up my hands and then some.

Her rose-tinted lips are quirked up in a bright smile that shows off all her white teeth, and before I know what the hell I'm doing, I find myself drawing closer when I should be working on finding my locker and my first period class.

A bell rings out through the air and the group collectively groans, saying their goodbyes and heading for their classes down the various hallways.

She must notice me standing here, staring at her like a creepy mindless fool because suddenly she turns, and our eyes meet. If I thought I was blinded by this girl before, I was wrong. Because her eyes are this incredible shade of purple, a deep amethyst with flecks of lavender and blue, so rare and unexpectedly stunning, I assume they are contacts.

They have to be. Eyes that gorgeous aren't real, but I sure as hell plan to paint them. I already know the colors I'll use.

She smiles at me and I smile back, wanting to say something to her, but not knowing what. She's still surrounded by a few lingering people, and I'm still the new kid who doesn't know anyone and doesn't fit into their world.

Her world.

She's clearly the queen bee and the queen never falls for the servant.

She tilts her head, her eyes flittering around my face and body as if she's trying to place me. Then she does the most amazing thing. She walks through the sea of people, heading directly for me. My heart stops dead in my chest before it slingshots into a sprint as if injected with a shot of adrenaline.

I can feel the color rising up my face, but I will myself to tamp it down as I straighten my spine and stare back unabashedly, the way she's staring at me.

"Hi," she says in a sweet melodic voice and my cock jumps in my khakis. "Are you new here?"

I open my mouth to answer her. To say yes and ask for her name. To tell her mine and ask what her schedule is because whatever hers is, I want to be in that class.

But before I can so much as utter a sound, one of her friends grabs her arm, throwing me a harsh look that suggests she's already onto me and isn't liking what she sees.

"See you around," she says to me as her friend drags her off and that's it. Moment over. But sure as hell not forgotten. Maybe this place won't be so bad after all.

Taking the lid off the stew, I give it a stir, rousing myself out of my reverie. I force myself not to think about the woman upstairs. The woman who is showering in my home and likely stuck here for a couple of days. Hopefully not longer. Hopefully this storm blows over quickly and her car is easy to fix, and she can be on her way. Hell, I have a truck and a SUV. She can take that.

I hardly even use it.

It's been well more than a year since Piper left. Since someone has been here, staying in this house with me. Even then, I never let Piper in my head or too deep in my heart. My walls were always up. Something I'm grateful for now considering one day she just decided she was done with me, the way everyone else has, and up and left.

Just like that.

I don't love you anymore, Miles, and was gone.

"Stop staring at the back of my head like that. It's for the best if she goes."

Betsy makes some kind of noise that doesn't take a dog whisperer to decipher she's huffing out a, who are you kidding, at me.

But what Betsy fails to understand is that's how my world makes sense. How everything fits and nothing breaks. London is London. Gorgeous face and curvy, fuckable body with a warm laugh sweet smiles, an incredible mind, and heart-stopping presence.

She is the package.

The one every boy imagines and conjures up in their heads as their ideal, perfect woman.

Really. She's it. Always has been.

Of all the people who had to crash their car and I had to happen upon, it had to be London.

I go about setting two bowls out. Two sets of silverware. I pop the top on a beer and wonder if I should open wine instead. Then I mentally shake myself. This isn't a date. This is not me trying to impress some woman.

London Canterbury is not and never will be mine.

I hear the bedroom door open and her feet along the hall upstairs. I go into the freezer and pull out an ice pack, cracking it so the inside of it breaks apart, and then I round the corner only to find her hobbling down the stairs.

Dammit. She's really hurting.

"Shit," I hiss, so pissed at myself for letting my need for distance from her overtake the help she requires. "I should have helped you up earlier. Are you in a lot of pain?" I race over to the stairs, jogging up the five or so steps she has left. Without thinking, I take her hand that's not holding on to the railing, and put it over my shoulder when what I really want to do is pick her up and carry her down, the way I did when she passed out in my arms earlier today.

"I took three ibuprofen. I'm sure that will help."

"I left you some stronger stuff there."

"Yeah, but if I take that on an empty stomach, they'll make me nauseated."

"Alright then. Lean your weight on me." She does and I do my best to ignore the scent of her freshly washed hair or the softness of the sweater she's wearing or the way her warm body feels when it's this close to mine. I crouch down so it's not a strain for her to reach my height and help her down the remaining steps.

"Thanks, Miles. You're really are quite the hero today, aren't you?"

"I'm trying to maintain my status as Captain America."

"With the glasses, you're also kind of like Superman."

"You mean Clark Kent."

"No," she huffs in some obvious discomfort. "Everyone knows he's always Superman. Like you."

I lead her over to the kitchen counter, helping her up onto one of the bar stools and pointing to the one next to it for her to put her leg up on. She's wearing flannel pajama pants, Christmas socks with reindeer grips on the bottom, and a cream-colored sweater. Her dark hair is still damp, hanging loosely down her back and over her shoulders, longer than it was even back in high school.

"Here. Some ice for your knee. Were you able to make your calls?"

She smiles gratefully at me and places it directly over her pajama pants while I go about finishing up dinner. "Yes. My dad was not happy as you can imagine until I told him who you were and then he backed down a bit."

"Who I am?"

"Someone I went to high school with. He was relieved that my rescuer is someone I know." I hear Betsy abandon her spot on her bed and come traipsing over to London. "Such a sweetie, aren't you?" she coos at Betsy. "What's…" She trails off with a laugh. "I don't even know if your dog's a girl or boy."

"Girl. Her name is Betsy," I tell her, glancing over quickly and meeting her eye before going back to the stove.

"Betsy. Interesting name for a dog."

"I didn't name her. She's a rescue dog. I adopted her from the shelter about a month ago."

I look over to find London smiling softly. "Hero indeed," she whispers softly, but I catch it as she rubs behind Betsy's ears.

I serve us our dinner, sitting in the seat on the other side of

London's leg instead of the one beside her. If this bothers her or not, she doesn't comment.

"Your home is beautiful, Miles. How long have you been living up here?"

"About five years," I tell her, and she nods, looking around. "When I bought it, it was a rundown farm, abandoned for close to a decade. But it had everything I needed, and the price was right, so I went for it."

"Did you restore it yourself?"

"Most of it."

She lifts her spoon loaded with stew up to her mouth, blowing on it before taking a bite. I watch, mesmerized, as she licks her lips and makes a humming noise in the back of her throat.

"Wow. Yum. This is really good. I'm not used to home cooking like this unless I'm at my parents' place, which isn't that often."

I'd cook for her every night if this were real.

"You said you live in the city? In New York?"

She peeks over at me with a wry smile flirting on her lips. "Did I say that?"

I chuckle, taking a sip of my beer. "Yeah. When you were lamenting your cell service provider."

"Oh, god," she groans, throwing her head back. "I forgot about that. Can we just pretend none of that happened? I blame it on the blood. I can't stand the sight of blood."

"You were fine."

She laughs. "You asked how hard I hit my head."

Crap. I might have. Not my best moment. "Then we'll pretend that didn't happen either. Do you want one?" I ask, holding up my beer. "I also have wine and some vodka in the freezer, I think."

"I'll stick to water for now. I might take one of those heavier pills later and I've already passed out once on your watch."

We eat in silence for a couple of minutes, a heavy, thick silence that I'm desperate to fill. I want to ask her a dozen questions. Learn what happened to her and her life after the bonfire.

It's a strange thing seeing a woman after so long who you used to be crazy about.

Who the last time you saw her, you were kissing her lips like you'd never have that shot again, before walking away.

It almost feels like we're stuck in some kind of unfinished business purgatory.

Because for me, that kiss didn't end when I walked away.

That kiss lasted me all through basic training. That kiss lasted me through a deployment and then even some time after. And not just because the kiss was incredible, which it was, but because of the girl. Her. The one I secretly pined over for three years before I finally worked up the balls to act, knowing nothing could come of it.

I was leaving and she was destined for things bigger and better than me.

But she kissed me back. Like she wanted it just as badly as I did, and that nearly ruined me. The regret for not acting sooner when I should have nearly destroyed me.

Still, I can't make myself ask those questions, even if to cut the somewhat awkward tension. I'm afraid of what the answers will do to me.

How learning about London Canterbury will feel knowing she's leaving the moment the snow clears and that I'll likely never see her again.

"What do you do up here, Miles?" she finally asks, breaking the silence the way I haven't been able to. "Are you a farmer? You said this was a farm."

"A farmer?" I laugh at the words. "No. Not a farmer, though I do own a tractor. I'm an artist. I make glass and metal pieces."

She pauses, her spoon in mid-air as she turns to study me, her eyebrows at her hairline. "For real?"

"It's actually why I bought the land. I turned the old barn into my workshop and now it's also a gallery where I sell pieces from."

"I saw a sign for that on the highway. Before I crashed that is."

"Yeah. Um… my ex had that part done. She's the one who turned half the barn into the gallery." And in truth, it was a genius move. I get a lot of foot traffic and sell pieces directly that way.

"I guess I shouldn't be surprised. You were always drawing and painting and sculpting."

Now it's my turn to be shocked.

"What? Why are you looking at me like that?" she asks.

"I just didn't realize you saw that."

She laughs, taking a sip of her water. "Miles, we had like almost every class together our junior and senior year. I took that art class I nearly failed that almost ruined my GPA. That and we had independent study together for all of senior year."

An independent study in creative writing I took for the sole reason that she was taking it.

I nod on a heavy swallow. I remember the art class, but that was class. That was controlled. Did she ever see some of the sketches I drew when I thought I was being so covert? I even still have some of them in a box in the basement somewhere.

Her. I sketched her. All the damn time. Like a creeper. A man obsessed.

She was my muse.

"I guess I didn't know you were paying attention."

Her eyes meet mine and something in them, in the knowing look she's giving me, has my heart jumping up in my chest. "When it came to you, I was always paying attention."

Chapter Six

MILES

Helping London over to the sofa, I set another log on the fire, stoking it a bit to kick it back up. "Can I run up and grab you one of the heavier pills?"

She scoots back, getting herself comfortable and gives me a sheepish look. "I feel like I'm taking advantage."

"Not even a little. Stop worrying about me. I wouldn't help if I didn't want to. One or two?"

"One. Definitely one."

I laugh at her horrified expression. Jogging up the steps, I walk into the guest room and then straight on into the bathroom, finding the bottle on the counter I have left over from when I had my wisdom teeth out in the fall. Beside her body lotion that I don't have to open to know smells like flowers and vanilla. Soft, feminine, and sweet. Like her.

I grab a pill from the bottle and close it back up, taking one last deep inhale because I can't help it, and then running back down. I hand her the pill and she takes it with water, thanking me once again.

I sit on the opposite side of the couch, about to ask her if she wants to watch a movie or some television when she says, "Can I ask you something?"

"Sure?" It comes out as a question when I don't intend it to, but it's the amusement in her eyes and the smirk on her lips that has me questioning if not a little relieved. I know she has bigger questions for me. I see them lingering on her, but I'm not ready to answer those. I don't think I'll ever be because once I open that dam, I'm not sure I'll be able to close it again.

"Well, I guess it's not really a question so much as an observation. I just didn't take you for the type of guy to like Taylor Swift."

I burst out laughing and she quickly follows, giggling and biting into her lip as she tries, and fails, to stifle it. "I'm not. It's for Betsy." London cocks an eyebrow and I shrug. "When I rescued her, the lady who runs the shelter told me Taylor Swift is the only thing that she'll listen to. It helps calm her down or something. Keeps her happy. She had a rough owner before me, and somehow this is what the shelter used to help her with that. I'm not even sure, but when I don't have it on, she seems tenser and since I've only had her a month and we're both still learning to trust each other, I play it for her. Half the time I don't even notice anymore."

"You play Taylor Swift to keep your *dog* happy?" London narrows her eyes, dumbfounded. "You must have women lined up around the block for you."

I mentally jar at that, completely taken aback. "Why would you say that?"

"Seriously?" she pushes incredulously, panning her hands at me and then around my house.

"What?"

She shakes her head, but this time she's studying me, and I don't like her scrutiny. "You don't see it, do you?"

My eyebrows knit together. I had my most recent ex and a few random women here or there, but most people, women especially, don't notice me. Never have.

London is proof of that.

"Never mind. I just think that's pretty incredible. Do you think Betsy will object if we watched a movie or something—"

Betsy starts barking, walking over to the door and scratching at it with vigor. I suppress a groan. "Alright, girl. I'm coming." I stand up, about to tell London we can put on a movie when I come back, but she stands as well, following me over to the front door. "You don't have to come with me. It's cold and snowing out. Plus your knee."

"I could use some fresh air."

I watch her for a moment, making sure she's okay. She was in an accident earlier, hitting her head, but she moves toward me effortlessly, hardly a limp in her step.

"Come here," I command on a resigned groan, watching as she drifts closer. When I found her earlier today, she wasn't wearing a coat. Or a hat or even gloves. I'm hoping they're all just packed in her suitcase, but I can't have her going outside in this weather dressed in a sweater and flannel pants.

Opening the front closet door, I pull my fleece on and tug a gray beanie over my head. Then I take my winter coat and throw it over her shoulders. It's several sizes too big, but it looks great on her.

"As adorable as you look dressed like a Christmas elf, I'd rather not have you freeze to death." I point to her boots and she steps into them as I grab a spare beanie and pull it down over her hair and hand her an extra set of my gloves that dwarf her hands as she slips them on.

She stares up at me and my breath stalls. "Ready?"

"Do I look like a lumberjack?"

I laugh, loving the glimmer in her eyes. "More like a firefly lost in a jar." She scrunches her nose at that, but the nickname, the one I've always secretly called her, forces a smug smirk to my lips.

Firefly.

My firefly.

The girl who always managed to light up my dark, bleak sky.

The second I open the door, a rush of freezing icy wind hits us. "Whoa. Damn. You weren't kidding about this storm."

I glance over my shoulder as I put Betsy's coat on her. "Change your mind about coming?"

"Nope. If you can brave it, so can I, superhero."

I chuckle lightly as I let Betsy go. She races forward, diving headfirst into the white stuff that isn't as powdery as it was the last time she did this. It's far more icy out and I know it's only a matter of time until we lose power.

I sigh thinking of that.

I have generators for a reason, but still. I worry about my studio.

London grasps my arm, a startled gasp escaping her lips in the form of a white plume of vapor.

"Betsy's fine," I reassure her. "She likes to do this. Loves the snow. Relax, she'll be back in no time." We step onto the porch, the light casting an eerie glow against the falling flakes. Visibility is shit and with this much snow and ice, it's going to take a while to fully clear it.

"Do you not see the wall of white?"

Oh, I see it. Reaching forward, I pick up a ball of it from the railing of the porch and chuck it at her chest. It splatters against my coat that's covering her and she jumps back with a squawk of surprised outrage.

"Hey," she snaps indignantly. "That's so unfair. I'm wounded."

"So that means you don't know how to throw a snowball?"

Her pretty eyes narrow, challenge glimmering like diamonds in the dark. "I played softball in high school."

I smirk. "I remember. But you played second base. Hardly known for their throwing prowess."

"So, that's how it is, huh?" She takes a step back, her smile meant to disarm me. It's working. "Did you think I'd cower?"

No. I knew she'd love this. It's why I started it. Anticipation buzzes a course of electricity through my veins. Wind whips past us, blowing her hair up and into her face and I take advantage, chucking another snowball, hitting her in the exact same place since I won't hit her face or head.

"I don't know. Looks like you're a bit slow to fight back." I laugh at her growl. "But like you said, you're injured."

"And drugged," she snaps. Before I can react, she grabs a chunk of snow and hurls it at me, hitting me directly in the face. "Oh, crap. Miles… I'm so…" But she's laughing too hard to get the full apology out.

I wipe my face of the cold icy slush she coated me in, flicking it to the porch. "It's like that, is it?"

She shakes her head, biting into her lip, but her words contradict her demure pose. "Bring it."

"Oh, firefly. You have no idea what you just asked for." I chuck a snowball right at her, hitting her square in the chest.

"You keep hitting me there. You're going to hurt my boobs."

"I can't hit your knee or your face. Turn around and I'll aim for your ass next."

She gasps out, going for her own weapon of snow, and without thinking twice, I leap forward, grasping her around the middle. She yelps, screaming out a laugh as I haul her against me, lifting her off her feet and spinning us around. My intent initially was to toss her into the snow, but at the last second, I remember the day she's had, the reason she's here, and try to back off.

But I'm starting to think those painkillers are kicking in and that maybe she is slightly drugged because before I can even comprehend what's happening, she's pushing her weight into me, tucking her mouth into my neck and… *blowing a raspberry*? I laugh out like a kid, shocked out of my mind, stumbling back a step as I try to push her away.

Only, I miscalculate how close I am to the edge of the porch and tip back, her still in my arms, and with her weight on my chest, we go down, falling backward. She screams as we go smashing into the bank of snow on the side of my porch that easily catches our fall. We're lucky to have it so high that we don't crash down the three steps that would likely break my ass if it were clear.

We land with an oomph, or maybe that's just me because I try to cradle London as much as possible, bearing the brunt of the impact. "London, are you okay? I'm so sorry. I shouldn't have done that." I shift to sit up, taking her with me and cupping her face in my gloved hands, checking her over.

Her eyes are on mine, but she's quiet, staring at me, and I can't discern her expression. Her eyes are a little heavy, probably from the drugs, as her gaze intensifies the longer she stares at me.

My heart starts to pound in my chest.

I don't even know what came over me. I've never done anything like that with anyone. I'm not playful.

"London?" I question, but it comes out strange. Strangled. A hoarse whisper as I gaze directly into her eyes. Eyes that are only inches from mine. She expels a breath, the white mist coasting over my lips and I lick mine intuitively.

Everything fades. The cold. The snow. The wind.

None of it registers as I look at her, thinking about how good her lips would feel on mine. Cold and full. But her tongue would be warm, her taste sweet, and I shiver at the thought of it. At the idea of kissing her again.

But just as that thought begins to spread like wildfire, something inside of me flips. Anguish suddenly crashes down on me, extinguishing the fire that had felt so consuming only seconds ago.

She's going to leave.

As everyone does.

Everyone leaves me and I can't... I don't want to fall in the shadow of her again.

I survived it once, but twice?

London clears her throat, still having not spoken, but with that sound I sit her up, pushing her away from me. Stupid for allowing myself to get as close as I did.

"London?" I repeat her name because now I'm starting to get worried.

She shakes her head ever so slightly as if clearing something from her mind and then she nods. "You didn't hurt me, Miles. But I think I'm going to go in. I'm cold. And suddenly very tired and my head is starting to feel foggy from the stuff I took."

I stand up, helping her do the same as we dust ourselves off, stepping back onto the porch. I'm going to have to snow blow this tomorrow, even if the storm continues, otherwise I'll never get ahead of it.

"If you wait a minute, I'll help you in and up the stairs."

"No," she says quickly, cutting me off and backing up toward the front door.

Dammit. I really messed up.

"I can manage. You wait for Betsy. Make sure she gets in safely." She pauses, looking back up at me and something in her expression causes me to reach for her only to have my hand drop just as quickly. "I'll see you in the morning, Miles. Sweet dreams."

I stare after her, unable to form the words to repeat her sentiment back to her. Because I already know I'm going to dream about her tonight. The sweetest dreams of them all.

Chapter Seven

LONDON

I think I had the filthiest dream last night. I'm blaming it on the drugs. And the heat in Miles's eyes last night as he stared into mine, looking like he wanted to kiss me.

No, not just kiss me… devour me.

I couldn't speak. Hell, I couldn't move. He was like the hottest thing ever, all big, strong muscles and bright blue eyes and huge smile like I've never seen on him before.

I think we can blame the dimples too. And his beard.

A beard I dreamt about tickling the sensitive skin between my legs as he brought me to orgasm over and over again. Even now, still, I'm squirmy and heated and wanting.

Too bad he doesn't want me back.

My eyes crack open slowly, my head heavy and my body slightly achy. I left the shades open on the window last night so I could wake up like this. I'm not sure if I was hoping for the storm to be over or not yet, but it's most definitely not over.

The sky is a dark, gloomy gray and the snow is coming down in what appears to be tiny white pebbles, blowing past the glass almost horizontally.

That's when I hear it.

The wind.

It roars and races through the siding of the house and down the chimney in the room I'm staying in. This room has a gas fireplace, unlike the massive wood one downstairs, but I was afraid to leave it on overnight.

I sit up slowly, taking stock of my body with each movement I make.

My knee still smarts, but not as bad as it did yesterday. Miles made me keep icing it and I'm grateful for that. I think it did a lot of good. My head is fuzzy and the cut on my hairline throbs, but I feel better today than I did yesterday, so that is a bonus.

Dangling my feet over the side, I look around the big, beautiful guest room and wonder if Miles is up or not.

Miles.

There is so much about that man that is unexpected. Maybe it's the fact that it's him who rescued me. The odds of such a wild thing happening.

He's not a big talker. And there is most definitely a darkness to him that I don't remember being there when we were younger. I didn't ask him about the kiss or about where he went after he walked away. Yesterday wrecked me. Shook me to my core. And as I sit in this warm, soft bed, listening to the storm outside the window, I keep thinking… what would have happened to me if Miles hadn't shown up?

It's a sobering thought.

Because I had hit my head and was bleeding. Because I had banged up my knee pretty good and could barely put weight on it, let alone walk. Because I had no cell service and no idea where the nearest anything was since it was not only a blizzard out, but we're pretty much in the middle of nowhere Vermont.

Scary stuff.

And I'm blaming my tiny crush on Miles as hero worship. It's certainly not related to us tumbling down in the snow and him staring at my lips like he was hungry for a taste only to flash revulsion and regret right after. That stung.

That's likely why I sat up awake, longer than I wanted last night, my mind filled with high school memories of him watching me when he didn't think I noticed or the way he did it again last night. The sketches he used to draw of me that he thought I never saw and how he makes art for a living now. Yup, my fan-girl crush has nothing to do with the fact that he once stepped in on a guy being a bit too aggressive with me and now lives in this gorgeous home with a rescue dog who will only listen to Taylor Swift, so he plays it for her.

He doesn't think I remember him, but I do.

I always remembered him.

I always saw him, even back then. Even when no one else did.

I shower in his gorgeous guest bathroom, deciding that later today I'm going to take a bath, and then change into a pretty black sweater that may or may not be on the tighter side and a pair of skinny jeans that may or may not hug my ass and thighs like they're painted on. I might also blow out my hair and apply some makeup, just enough so that it looks like I'm not wearing any, but my skin is glowing, and my eyes are a little shimmery, and then I open the door to head downstairs.

Before I can make it very far, I hear him talking to Betsy and whatever he's cooking up smells fantastic. Like bacon and eggs and pancakes and my stomach growls like I haven't eaten in a hundred years. Which may be since I don't cook much in the city—I have a tiny kitchen in my apartment—and my female friends don't eat anything that could be construed as a carb or fat.

But it's the way he's talking to his dog that's giving me pause.

The sweet, gentle tone he uses with her while speaking to her as if she's a human who can read his mind. It has me smiling like crazy as I creep along the long open-air hall that overlooks the great room downstairs. I can't see his kitchen as it's off to the side, but I don't have to. His voice carries, bouncing off all the hard surfaces this place is comprised of.

Betsy barks and I hear him making a tsking sound. "I already gave you two pieces of bacon. Don't stand there barking at me when you've had more than you already should have." She barks again and I hear him groan. "Okay. Last piece and I mean it. After this, you can eat your eggs and potatoes and like it." Silence ensues and I tread carefully, still not wanting to interrupt this most adorable moment. But then Betsy barks again, this one sounding different and I hear him say, "She'll be down soon, girl. But don't get too attached to having her here. She'll be gone before you know it."

And that's the moment that I stop dead in my tracks, a frown tracking down my face.

He's not saying anything untrue or even mean, but it's his tone. The cold indifference of it and I instantly go back to the way he looked at me last night before I tucked tail and ran in the house. He's doing all these things for me because he's a nice man with a big heart, an obvious caretaker, but he does not want me here.

I blow out a sigh of disappointment at that.

I haven't had a boyfriend in a while. I'm what you call in the city a serial dater and that's not because that's what I enjoy. It's because dating in New York City is the equivalent of working in a health center. You're always screening for the mentally unstable ones, STIs, and people who have the potential to hurt you or run out without paying.

I didn't come up with that pearl, my friend Rina did and since she's a nurse in a health center, she's allowed to say things like that. But I think it's kind of true. Dating in the city is all about apps that show faces and bodies and are a mechanism for hooking up and not connecting.

I can't remember the last time I connected with anyone.

Last night wasn't a date, but it was the best first date I've had in a while if for no other reason than the guy didn't talk about himself all night and only care about how fast he could get into my pants.

I make my appearance known as I step noisily onto the stairs. Miles comes around the corner and looks up at me, his eyes full of concern as they do a sweep of my body. But his gaze starts to drag. Starts to linger. Starts to grow a little heated as he takes in my full appearance instead of just focusing on my injuries and physical limitations.

"Good morning," I say to him, taking him in much the way he

did me. He's wearing another thermal shirt that is just as affectionate with his body as my jeans are with me. This time it's navy blue and it makes his eyes glow bright. His hair is brushed back off his face, and his jeans are low-slung, clinging on for dear life to his trim waist.

His is a sight a girl could grow very used to.

"Morning," he drawls in return, a little something extra in his voice as his gaze finally finds its way back up to mine. "How are you feeling? You certainly look good."

"Are you flirting with me?"

He chuckles, glancing away and running a hand through his hair and mussing it all up. Now it's a hot mess and I'm dying to fix it with my fingers. He's not wearing his glasses today, I note, and I can't remember if he was wearing them when he found me yesterday either.

"It seems I am." He shakes his head and then turns back to me, his smile gone as he returns to his stoic self. "Are you hungry? And yes, that's me changing the subject."

I smile down at him. My good smile. The one I use when I meet people I want to charm. But it also feels like I've got a secret, my dirty dream front and center in my mind. "I'm starving and if it tastes half as good as it smells, I might have to fight Betsy for that bacon."

He mutters something I can't hear under his breath. "Do you need help down?"

"Naw. I'm good."

And I am. I mean, it still hurts to walk, especially down the stairs where I constantly have to bend and then straighten my knee, but I can't use that as an excuse to fawn all over him.

I make it to the bottom and he's there, waiting on me.

His eyes are still on mine and mine are still on his, and I watch as his face inches closer. As his eyes darken ever so subtly. His lips nearly brush my cheek as they reach my ear, whispering, "You're a terrible liar. You limped the whole way down."

My breath catches as his warm breath fans across my skin, his body so close as his heat and masculine scent envelop me. But just as quickly as he was there, he draws back, our eyes clashing as he shifts his position, coming to stand beside me.

"I did not limp."

"You did. Humor me and put your arm around my shoulder. Like we did it last night." And those words after all the dirty places my mind was going is not helping anything. I silently do as he instructs while he helps me over to the breakfast bar. "Put your leg up. I'm thinking your knee could use some more ice and I'll make you a plate."

The second he gets me into my chair and steps away, I hear him expel a breath, see him unclenching his fists that I hadn't even realize he was clenching. But his jaw is still tense as he goes to the freezer to retrieve my ice pack.

"The weather is looking pretty rough out there," I comment, hoping to alleviate some of the tension I feel building between us.

No sooner are the words out of my mouth then the lights flicker.

My eyes pop open wide, searching around the room to make sure we do still in fact have power.

"It's not supposed to stop until tomorrow afternoon. Then it will likely take a day or so for everything to be fully plowed out." He turns to me, watching my expression carefully as he creates a mammoth plate that could feed a grizzly. "And yes, we'll likely lose power as the wind is supposed to kick up some more. But relax. I have a generator that runs on natural gas and plenty of wood for the fire. We'll be fine."

"Right." I glance down, my hands twisting in my lap. "You didn't exactly plan on me for your Christmas guest though."

He marches toward me, plate in hand, setting it on the counter and placing the ice on my knee. His hand cups my face, lifting my chin until I'm forced to meet his steady gaze. "I wasn't planning on anyone for my Christmas guest, so that makes no difference to me. I'm just sorry that you likely won't make it in time for Christmas Eve with your family."

And before I can stop myself, I ask, "Who are you spending Christmas with?"

He releases my face, turning away from me and heading back

into the kitchen, making himself busy as he places a strong helping of distance between us. "Betsy. But I usually work Christmas since no one comes through and the gallery is closed. It's a good day to get stuff done."

My heart jerks at that. I wonder who Miles has in his life. If he's as alone as he appears to be.

Just as I'm lifting my first bite of eggs to my mouth, the lights flicker, then go out, and don't come back on. "Miles," I whisper.

"Wait for it."

A loud mechanical sound clicks on and with it, some of the lights, but not all of them.

"We'll have heat?" I ask.

"In some spots of the house, yes. We'll still have hot water. The stove works, as does the microwave and toaster, but the oven is out. Half the lights down here and I think the lights in your bedroom don't work either. Just in your bathroom. Much of the back of the house won't have heat or a lot of power."

"The back of the house?" My eyebrows tilt in.

"Eat up," he says to me. "I need to check on the gallery and my studio to make sure the other generator clicked on there too."

"You can go if you need to. I can certainly eat here by myself."

He shakes his head. "I want to show you around a bit. There is something I think you'll really like."

Chapter Eight

MILES

"You look sad," I comment, feeling the matching frown on my own face.

She chews her piece of pancake like she's trying to set a record on speed. Then she shrugs.

"What is it? Not being with your family?"

She swallows audibly, taking a hasty sip of her coffee. "I'm not sad."

"Do you remember what I said about you being a bad liar?"

She huffs out an aggravated sound. "Fine. I'm a little sad. It's just that Christmas is my favorite holiday. The lights. The music. The movies and homemade cookies. And yes, it's also the holiday we always spend together as a family."

Fuck. I have none of that. And with the power out and the oven gone, I can't even bake her cookies. Not that I even know how because I've never done that before. Cooking I can do, but baking is something else altogether.

"I see your wheels spinning, Miles, and that was not my intention. I'm good. I swear, I am. I don't want to sound like a downer or come off as ungrateful because I'm not. I'm really glad I'm here with you."

Her eyes burn into mine with a sincerity that has me rubbing absently at a sore spot on my chest.

"What's your favorite Christmas movie?"

"What's yours?" she throws back at me.

"I don't do holidays, London. Just tell me and we can watch it together later if you want."

"*Christmas Vacation.*"

"Done."

She lets out a small sigh, returning to her breakfast and I turn away from her, going about doing the dishes. The dishwasher is out too, so I have to do everything by hand, grateful for the busy work that allows me to ignore the woman in my home.

I didn't get a lot of sleep last night. I laid awake, tossing and turning, thinking about her. Thinking about her only being down the hall from me, sleeping in my home. I had lost myself with her last night in the snow and I regret it.

That certainly wasn't helping me get a restful sleep.

It's been eight years since I last saw London, but seeing her now, spending time with her, it's like something out of a dream. A reality I never imagined possible when I left.

It's a daunting thought.

Scary as hell because being with her, it's as if no time has passed.

The first, the *only*, girl I… loved.

I thought about what it would be like with her over the next couple of days, here with me only because of the storm and with no other reason to stay. She wants to leave. To spend Christmas with her family and I don't blame her for that.

But that doesn't mean I want her to go either.

It's a funny realization that hit me harder than I expected.

Which is why I'm determined to keep her out. To not let the girl I fell for the moment I saw her all those years ago, lure me in the way only she can.

I have enough regrets when it comes to London Canterbury.

I finally managed to fall asleep, telling myself it's only a couple of days. That if I keep myself in check, then she can't dig into me too deep.

Then I saw her at the top of the stairs this morning and realized I'm already such a fucking mess with this woman.

I think I always have been.

She never went away.

Like pausing your favorite song, knowing that when you hit play again, it'll all come rushing back word for word and note for note.

London finishes her breakfast quickly and I lead her through the rest of the first floor which she didn't get to see last night. The renovations on this part of the house, leading out to the barn took the longest and the most money. Well, the most other than building my studio so I wouldn't have to rent space or time in an open studio.

Once we reach the back of the house, stepping down into the solarium, she gasps as I knew she would. This room is my oasis. My ex thought it was a waste at the time. But I had just sold a huge light installation for a lot of money, and at the end of the day, it was my house and my call.

"Miles," London says on an awed whisper, walking slowly into the center of the glass room. The wall on the left is dark planked wood with a large fireplace in the center. But everything else, the two other walls and the entire ceiling are glass panes. The roof was the hardest part. The skylights are five panes thick each to accommodate for their size and the weight of any snow. They're sloped, but I've had to shovel them off a few times since this room was finished.

"Do you like it?"

"Like it?" She laughs incredulously, spinning around with a beaming smile before turning back to the room. "I love it. It's incredible. I don't think I've ever seen anything like it."

Her hand touches everything as she takes in the room. Every surface. Before she stops at the large French doors that lead out to the patio and the grounds beyond.

"How much land do you own?"

"Ten acres. Most of it is wooded, so I don't have to do much with that."

The snow is dropping from the sky and all around us is a sea of white. The skylights are completely covered, and I wish she were able to see what it's like here in the spring, when everything is starting to bloom. All the colors that come with it.

Then I mentally kicked my own ass for those thoughts, repeating my mantra about distance, though it feels like it's giving me the finger while laughing at me.

"The problem with this space is that it's not heated by the generator as it's in the back of the house and with all the glass, requires too much of a pull. When I had to make cuts to heat and power the necessities, this room hit the list."

"I can feel that," she says on an exaggerated shudder, wrapping her arms around herself. "Maybe I can come back here later though?" She turns back to me with a tilt of her head, those violet eyes reaching places I wished she didn't have access to. "Use the fireplace and bring a blanket? I'd love to sit here and write. God" — she shakes her head— "I'd write all the books if I had a room like this."

Despite my best efforts, I smile.

Kinda fucking big actually.

Because for some reason, when she told me what she does for a living, I pictured her here, sitting at the wood dining table off to the right or curled up on the sofa in front of the fire or lounging on the chaise, staring out at the nature beyond the room and writing her stories.

I love the fact that London is an author. It's so perfect for her.

She used to write stories for our independent study, and I'd watch as she would get so into them. Her face always filled with concentration or secret smiles or deep frowns as she would write. Her face was full of expression and I watched because I was always watching her when she wasn't looking.

Studying the real London.

Not just the popular princess, but the one I saw beneath.

"We can do that. We can definitely do that." I need to stop smiling. I need to stop staring into her eyes. But most of all, I need to stop imagining things I should not imagine with her. "I'd like to show you my workshop first. That, and I have to check it. It runs on a separate generator. A much larger, industrial one, and I have some things cooling in my ovens, so if they're without power, I'm in some trouble."

"Will you show me how you make glass?" She scrunches up her nose. "That's not how you say it, I'm sure, but I'd love to watch you do it or even try it out myself." She throws her hands out defensively. "As long as I won't ruin anything or be in your way."

"You're not in my way and as long as you're careful, you won't ruin anything."

"What is this?" she asks as we enter the long, closed-in breezeway.

"It's what leads to the barn. I had to enclose it because of weather like this." I pan my free hand out to the side, indicating the storm beyond the windows.

We reach the door and I smile down at her, wanting to put my mouth back by her ear, to whisper into it and watch her shudder against me. But I hold off. "This is my space."

I open the door and we enter my large rectangular barn. The floors are cement in this part, and I have a huge flaming fire pit set up with a large glory hole in it. There are several steel tables, wooden stools and posts, buckets of mallets and instruments.

It's my heaven. My haven.

It's where I come when I need to space out and think and create.

Blowing glass is not easy. It's a multifaceted work of art that often requires several steps and instruments and has left me more burns than I care to think about. I have a few pieces I'm particularly fond of cooling in the long-term oven. If they lose power and the ovens don't restart, then those pieces risk cracking or shattering.

"Miles," London draws in a sharp breath, glancing up at me with wide eyes before she returns to what I have out. She picks up a clear glass globe, filled with pink and blue glittery pieces. "You made this? An ornament?"

"Yes. I make a lot of them this time of year. Many custom but this is one of my best sellers."

She twirls it around in her hand, her eyes wide as the flakes of color tumble with her movements. She looks up, well beyond this space, far off to the other side of the massive barn where you can see the gallery, filled with pieces for sale as well as catalogs of larger items to order.

It's dark in here now, most of the light only coming in from the windows as a lot of the overhead lights aren't on the generator to make up for the amount of power the ovens and fire draw.

"It's beautiful. Wow." She sets down the ornament, walking across the room, her hands behind her back almost as if she's afraid of touching anything. I stand back, watching her take in my space. She comes upon a glass sculpture I have sitting in sand. It's cooled and set, I just haven't moved it to the gallery yet. She looks to me, her expression curious and questioning, and I nod my head. She picks it up carefully, holding the piece in one hand, and delicately runs her fingers over the fine lines of colored glass. "It's exquisite."

"Thank you," I say, a strong surge of pride rushing through me. I was nervous to show this to her. Her opinion of me and the things I make is already more important than it should be.

I snap myself out of my trance and get to work, checking the ovens and the items I have cooling in there.

"You have a lot of power in this space," she comments, coming to stand beside me, trying to peek inside.

"I have a different generator for here than I do for the main house. A lot bigger and more powerful."

"Can we make a piece together? I'd like you to show me how you do this?"

I shut the doors to the oven and turn to her. "What would you like?"

She glances toward the ornament that's back on the table. "Can we make one of those?"

"What color?"

Her eyes flash up to mine, staring thoughtfully. "Navy blue?"

I chuckle, stepping forward. Reaching up, I capture a wayward piece of her dark hair, brushing it off her face and tucking it behind her ear. My hand lingers for a moment as I stare back into her eyes. Eyes that make my chest clench.

Or is it the woman doing that?

"What about violet?" I already know the perfect color combination.

"What about red? For Christmas."

"Red it is then." My eyes bounce around her face and I don't remember wanting to kiss a woman this badly since her. The way I did so long ago. The last imprint of London Canterbury I have and now here she is. "Clear or opaque?" I ask, forcing myself to step back and away from her as I go in search of some red glass pillows from the large storage unit I have.

"Um. Clear?"

"Just a round ball and do you want to put something in it?"

"Yikes. All these questions. What are my choices?"

I glance over my shoulder at her. "Anything you want, really. But you can think about it. First, we have to make the orb. I can change the shape depending on what you want, but if you want to put something inside it, there aren't as many choices." I pull out what I need, showing her what's in my hand.

"I think just the ball is good. Keep it simple."

"These are glass pillows." I hold open my hand for her to see and she reaches out, her fingers caressing one of the pieces. "All glass is made up of sand." She dips her head like she already knows this. "These pillows are basically crushed pieces of glass with color already infused into them. It's a hell of a lot easier and quicker to do it this way than to make colored glass from scratch because in order to get the right color, you often need to use different transition metals and depending on what they are, they can either be a bit dangerous to work with or insanely expensive to procure and then work in."

"Transition metals? Like what?"

"Iron, cobalt, silver, palladium, mercury, gold, the list goes on."

"Mercury?"

I laugh at her expression. "Yeah. Now you know why I purchase them as pillows. But really, they come in any color you can think up and you can purchase them already infused with specific metals if you're going for a particular look. For this, we're using basic red. Do you want to put them into the fire through what we call the glory hole while I go over to get my blowpipe?"

"Glory hole? Blowpipe?" she snorts out, taking the red pieces from my hand and doing exactly as I instruct her. "That sounds seriously dirty."

"Just wait till I put my long rod in it."

She turns to look at me with wide eyes, a blush creeping up her face. I wink at her as I pick up my blowpipe, showing it to her.

"It's certainly long, but it's a bit on the thin side."

"If you want it thicker, I'd be happy to accommodate."

I watch as her breath hitches and the pink in her face grows warmer, sexier, her eyes darkening at the blatant suggestion in my voice. Blood roars through my veins, making my cock twitch. I force myself to move back, already teetering on an edge I shouldn't be anywhere near.

"I think we're just about ready to start."

She clears her throat. "What's next?"

"Come here and I'll show you."

Chapter Nine

MILES

"That is so cool!" she says as I pull some of the molten glass onto the end of my blowpipe, rolling it around on the steel table so I can start to form it. I put it back through the glory hole to heat it and then remove it again, angling it down toward the ground so it can elongate.

"Come here," I tell her, tucking myself in beside her, my chest to her back and arm. "Put your mouth here and blow."

"You want me to blow on your pipe?"

You have no idea. "Come on, I bet you're great at it." I fight my grin as her eyes dance between amused, shocked, and panicked. I nod in encouragement and she places her mouth where I tell her to and blows hard before I quickly cap it off and put it back in the fire.

"Why do you keep doing that? Putting it back in the fire?"

"So it doesn't ball up or become unworkable. You ready to blow some more?"

"Are you intentionally being dirty or is this just glass blower lingo?"

"Both. You're fun to watch blush."

"Or maybe you just like that I have a dirty mind."

I stifle a groan. "Probably a lot of both. No more dirty talk, firefly, or you'll distract me, and we'll mess this all up. Or worse, burn ourselves."

"That can happen?"

"Oh, it can happen. I have a few nice scars I can show you later."

"And that's not meant to be dirty? You showing me your… scars?"

I cock a brow, my mouth curling up into a sly grin. "You do have a dirty mind. I'm not sure I knew that about you before."

"It's not exactly something I was flaunting in high school. Glad I can keep you on your toes though, Miles."

Can't argue that.

We repeat the procedure before I score the end and roll the ball with a wet wooden mallet. "Here." I take her hand, helping her to place the piece back in the fire, showing her how to spin it at the right speed so it doesn't alter the shape we just created. "You're good at this. A natural."

"Well, if writing doesn't pan out, maybe you can hire me on as a lackey."

"Apprentice. We call them apprentices."

"Is that a fancy term for unpaid help?"

"Something like that."

She does it a few more times, but I can practically feel her curious gaze back on me.

"You called me firefly again."

I pause, staring into the flames through the glory hole, blinking a couple of times before I take the pipe from her and finish off the spinning. "I hadn't realized. Sorry."

"I like it. Did you just come up with that last night?" From the tone of her voice, I get the impression she knows I didn't.

"No," is all I say as I pull the ball out of the fire and score it some more. "Tap the rod right here."

"Thought not. You sure you want me to do that?" She juts her chin toward the end of the pipe and the piece of glass sitting on it.

I laugh. "I'm positive."

She taps on the rod and the red glass ball drops onto the sand pile and she lets out a small squeal of delight. "Oh my god. It's so beautiful." She bends in half, studying it and thankfully smart enough not to touch it. Her head tilts as her eyes narrow. "But it has a hole." She turns her head over her shoulder to meet my eye. "How do we fill it?"

I bark out a laugh and wink at her. "Watch and I'll show you."

She grins, her enthusiasm infectious. Playful, dirty London is quickly becoming one of my favorite looks on her.

Pulling out my blowtorch, her eyes turn into twin saucers. "Step back," I instruct, meeting her deer in headlights gaze. "Last chance to put something in it. And no, that was not a sexual reference."

She shakes her head. "Can we leave it like this? It's so pretty."

I heat the end and add on some clear molten glass, twisting it and forming the loop that will attach with a string on to a tree.

"Done," I tell her, putting the torch away.

"That's it?"

"Almost. Put on these gloves and we'll place it in the long-term oven so it can slowly cool, otherwise we risk it cracking or shattering."

Her small hands slide into my large gloves and then she picks up the completed piece, following after me and setting it where I show her. We close the doors and when I turn to face her, she's all smiles. Her skin is slightly tacky with sweat, same as mine, from the heat of the fire and the glass, and I have the strongest urge to reach up and wipe some of it from her face.

Bring it to my lips and taste her saltiness on my tongue.

"When will it be ready?"

"About two days or so. If you're already gone, I can ship it to you."

She frowns slightly, nodding her head and turning away from me. I said that more for me than for her—an ugly reminder of our situation.

She looks around, taking in each piece of equipment with curiosity and interest.

"That was so much fun. Where did you learn how to do that?"

"I had taken a few classes in high school and loved it, but after I got out of the army——"

"You were in the army?" she interrupts, spinning around at light speed to face me, her voice shrill.

My eyebrows pinch and I nod slowly, tilting my head as I take her in. Confused by her response.

"Is that where you went? What happened to you?"

"What?"

She blows out a breath, looking up to the exposed beam ceiling as if she's struggling with something before she rights herself and stalks over to me with angry determination. "I haven't brought it up, Miles. I wasn't sure how and I didn't want to make this weird or awkward." She wags her finger back and forth between us. "But you called me firefly. The same thing you called me right before you kissed me graduation night. You marched across that field, your eyes on me, and then you kissed the hell out of me only to walk off immediately after without so much as a word. Then you were gone." She shoves at me and I'm so stunned, I take a step back. "I went looking for you. The next morning, I went to your house, but you weren't there and the woman who answered the door...your mother?"

I shake my head and she throws her hands up.

"She said you were gone with all your stuff and that you weren't coming back. That was it, Miles. You were gone and I never heard from or saw you again."

"You came looking for me? Why?"

She lets out a sardonic laugh. "Because I couldn't get that goddamn kiss out of my head. I was mad at you. Mad because you hadn't done it before when I had always..." She trails off, whirling around and putting her back to me as her hands hit her hips.

I step to her, turning her back around to face me and staring into her eyes from inches away. "Always what?"

She swallows hard, losing some of her anger and fight as her eyes bounce back and forth between mine. "You left," she whispers.

My hand comes up, cupping her jaw, my thumb skirting along her soft flesh and something inside of me stirs back to life.

"I had to."

"You could have told me." I shake my head and the frustration is back in her eyes and she shoves me away. "Why did you kiss me then if you were leaving and not coming back?"

Part of me wants to tell her. To lay my cards on the table.

But for what purpose?

If I give in to London the way she's asking, there will be no coming back from that. She will own me, as she always has. I will be at her feet and I… I can't let that happen.

Maybe that makes me a coward, but there is only so much loss a man can take in his life and London could easily be the worst of all if I let her.

"Please, Miles," she whispers, her hand touching my chest, her eyes beseeching. "Please tell me."

Shit…

I blow out a ragged breath. "She wasn't my mother. The woman who answered the door. She was my foster mother and I was eighteen. She was no longer being paid by the state to keep me. I was working two jobs to make up for that so I wouldn't be homeless and buy myself food and art supplies. I had enlisted in the army because I knew that was the best place for me to go if I wanted a real chance at life. I wasn't going to New York with you, London. There was no ivy league in my future. You have always been a million miles apart from me and I knew it."

Her eyebrows knit together, her body leaning closer to mine, deeper into my chest. "Then why——"

A growl sears past my lips, a hand running through my hair. Fuck it.

"Because I couldn't leave without saying goodbye to you. I thought about it. Debated it. I knew nothing could come of anything with you. But when I saw you standing there, sipping on your drink and having a quiet moment, I needed to do more than just say goodbye. I had to kiss you because I had wanted to kiss you for three years and if I was never going to see you again, then I had nothing left to lose."

Tears leak over the edges of her eyes and I brush them away, bringing my hands back up to her face. Her breath hitches and she looks so sad. I want to kiss it all away. London Canterbury should never know from sadness.

"I didn't know you were living in foster care."

"No one did."

"You could have told me."

"Tell you what? That my dad died when I was eight. That my mom decided when he died she didn't want to be my mother anymore and left because she couldn't handle looking at me and remembering him? That's not exactly the story you go around telling people. Especially in a high school like the one we went to."

"Jesus, Miles," she says on a sob. "You're wrong about us. We were friends. At least that's what I considered us. Did you mean what you just said?"

"Which part?"

"That you had wanted to kiss me for three years?"

My thumb skirts over her bottom lip, my eyes staring down, watching the motion, before I find her eyes again. "Since the moment I saw you."

She lets out a humorless laugh. "Well then, I wish you had done it earlier. Because I sure as hell had wanted you to."

"You did?" I stare at her incredulously.

She nods slowly, her eyes on me and her swallow heavy. I lean into her, our faces inches apart and our eyes fused as one. My heart thunders in my chest.

A warning to step back.

This woman. This beautiful, incredible woman who makes me laugh and smile when I haven't in years—maybe not ever—blows back into my life with the force of a wrecking ball, hellbent on total destruction.

I lean in farther, our noses practically touching, and I hear her take a deep breath. I follow the way she licks her lips. I catch the hint of toothpaste and the sweetness of the maple syrup she poured all over her pancakes on her breath.

"Firefly," I whisper inches from diving into the heaven that is her mouth, just as a loud bark startles us apart like two teenagers caught in the act.

London takes a step away from me, her eyes dropping down to Betsy because she's safe territory and I'm not. I was seconds away from devouring her, consequences be damned, and she knows it. But then London giggles, shaking her head and biting into her lip, her eyes lavender and playful, all traces of lust washed away, and I chuckle because what else is there to do.

Cock-blocked by my dog. So typical.

Running a frustrated hand through my hair, I try to catch my breath. I meet London's steadfast gaze and reality hits me square in the chest.

She's not mine to kiss.

"We should go back to the house," I tell her, my voice growing an edge I wish wasn't there, but am powerless to hide. Because the truth is, if we stay here, I'm going to kiss her. And then where will I be when she leaves?

Chapter Ten

LONDON

Miles leads me through the long, enclosed breezeway—can it be called a breezeway if it's enclosed?— back to the main house. We're silent and I'm not sure what the hell is going on. I wanted him to kiss me. Just the thought of it made my toes curl and my knees weak and my nipples hard and my stomach dip.

And that was just the *thought* of his lips on mine.

But I have to wonder at the wisdom of giving into this.

Is it nostalgia? Unfinished business? Are those the reasons that I find I want this guy like I haven't wanted a man in I don't even remember how long? I mean, how does that even make sense? I've been here only twenty-four hours and to add to that, I haven't seen him in eight years, and suddenly I'm dying to climb him like one of those big trees out there?

I don't know, but there you have it, folks.

We enter the solarium that is like something out of my dreams. I wasn't kidding when I told him I could live in this room and never want to leave. If it had a bathroom and maybe a small fridge, I never would. I stepped foot in here and my mind raced. My fingers itched.

All I wanted to do was sit down, watch the snow fall, and write.

I finished up my last novel that is now sitting pretty with my editor, so I'm free to start something new.

This.

I could write this.

A woman who gets stranded and is rescued by a guy she crushed on throughout high school. Only now, that guy is a totally hot artist. With big muscles. And an adorable smile. And gives the most steamy, panty-melting stares ever.

A laugh bubbles its way up through my chest, pausing on my lips in the form of a crazy smile.

"You okay?" Miles asks, side-eyeing me with a strange expression.

I nod, still unable to rein in my smile. "Yup."

"Really? 'Cause you look a little manic again."

Now that laugh explodes, only proving his point further. "Don't be rude." I nudge into his arm with my shoulder because I want to touch him and he's tall and yeah, maybe I'm slightly manic. It's either this room or the almost kiss.

No way to be certain.

"Did you want me to light a fire in here?" he questions as we enter the solarium which is at the end of the breezeway thing. "You said you wanted to do that. Sit in here and write, but now it's really cold. I can grab you a blanket and I have a space heater I can drag in here too."

My feet pause and I turn to look at Miles.

It's freezing in here. He wasn't kidding and a fire and a space heater and even a blanket would be amazing. But first, I think I need to ask him something. Call it research or morbid curiosity, but I can't stop the words as they tumble out.

"Why did you wait until that night at the bonfire?"

Miles blows out a breath as he looks past me, his expression grim, watching Betsy's retreating form run up toward the warmer, heated part of the house. But then silence descends upon us and part of me wants to take it back.

To tell him never mind, it's cool.

But I can't make the words form because it's not cool. I need to know.

That one kiss…

"London," he says my name on a pained whisper. I don't move. I wait. My breath held deep in my lungs as he works out whatever it is he's trying to work out inside that mind of his. "You had boyfriends. Were cheer captain. Went to parties. Had a million friends. You were the most popular girl in school, London Canterbury, and I was…" He huffs out a weighted breath, running his hand through his hair as he always seems to whenever frustration or agitation gets the better of him. "You were everything and at the time, I believed I was nothing. I had no parents, not even my mother wanted me. I had no home. No money. No real friends. You were nice to me, but you were nice to everyone. You were a fantasy I knew could never come to life and I…"

"What?" I push when he doesn't follow that up because the bastard just called me a freaking fantasy.

"I had no confidence. To me, it was easier to want you from afar than to risk trying something and you rejecting me. That would have killed me. I'd already been rejected enough."

God. His words make me want to find his mother and smack the bitch. I get grief and heartache, but I do not get abandoning your child the way she did. An eight-year-old boy.

I want to kiss him.

So insanely bad, I want that.

I want to take away his pain and fill it up with so many beautiful, special things. Show him just how special and amazing he is and that anyone who was indifferent to that is the one missing out, not him.

But then what happens after I do that?

His vulnerability is written all over his face and this is a man who does not wear vulnerability well.

Even so, now is not the moment to push that. It will come off as pity and I'd rather die than do that to such a strong man. So instead, I step into him, wrapping my arms around his waist and tucking my head against his chest. His heart is pounding against my ear and I smile.

He stiffens at first, like a wood freaking log, until finally he softens, and his arms find my back, holding me against him.

"I'm glad it was you yesterday," I whisper, smiling just a little bigger. "It would have been really awkward staying at a stranger's house through this storm."

He chuckles, which was of course my intent.

"It could have been like *The Shining*."

I give an exaggerated shudder and he laughs harder.

"You crazy people who live in the woods in the snow really should get your heads checked." I step back, winking at him and making a show of looking out the window at the beauty beyond it. "I mean, how you tolerate all this stunning nature and gorgeous wildlife and beautiful dream home is beyond me."

"Oh?" he challenges, cupping my chin and turning my face back to his. "So, you're saying that living in an apartment with neighbors surrounding you, in a cockroach-infested city with smog and traffic and constant noise is the way to go?" He makes a tsking sound in the back of his throat. "Damn. And all this time I had it wrong with the stunning nature, gorgeous wildlife, and beautiful dream home."

I sink my teeth into my lip as I try to fight my smile. "The restaurants are really good."

His face grows serious as his eyes search my face. "My cooking is better."

His cooking is really good.

"The shopping can't be beat."

"We have designer outlets not too far away."

"Then I guess Vermont has everything New York doesn't," I muse with a quirk of my lips.

He shakes his head, his expression deliberate. "Not everything." I swallow my tongue at the way he says that. "I'm going to start the fire. Why don't you grab your laptop."

Right. My laptop. Work.

I spin on my heels and race out of here, passing Betsy who is contentedly gnawing away on a bone, and up the stairs, ignoring the ache in my knee.

Wowzers, Miles Ford is intense.

So intense I feel his damn intense eyes in the pit of my stomach. I've had a very serious and active case of butterflies since I woke up yesterday on his couch and if he keeps this stuff up, I'm libel to start throwing them up.

I go for my phone, wishing, praying I have service here. Miles seems to on his cell, so what the fuck? Doesn't the world understand that I could really use a phone-a-friend moment about now? Rina or I'd even settle for my sisters, who would likely roll around on the floor laughing or just tell me to take the bull by the horns, or his balls in my hand, knowing them, and kiss him.

"Rina," I growl as I pick up my phone seeing that it blatantly shows no service. "You can't move to Boston. I need you, dammit!"

I need her blunt truths because within the span of twenty-four hours, my mind and my heart are going in some wild, uncharted places.

Grabbing my laptop from its case, I do my best to calm myself back down.

But god! I can't get all the things he said this morning out of my head.

Making my way back downstairs, I enter the solarium to find a fire roaring in the large fireplace, a space heater off to the side cranked up, the large white down comforter I woke up in yesterday, and a spread of cheese, fruit, crackers, nuts, and wine on the coffee table.

"How long was I upstairs?"

Miles glances up from his perch on the far corner of the sofa, his knees bent with a sketchpad resting against them, his right hand poised with some kind of thick, dark pencil in it. He smiles and my chest flutters right on cue. "I just figured you might be hungry."

Could this man be any more thoughtful? "If you keep this up, you'll make it impossible for me to leave when this storm blows over."

His gaze holds mine as he says, "Maybe that's my plan."

He immediately returns to his sketchpad, leaving me standing here in the middle of the room without a retort, trying to absorb what he just said.

Miles has this way about him. A bluntness that is new to me and never fails to make me squirm in my shoes. Did he mean that? He wants me to stay?

I can't even with that right now and he clearly wasn't looking to start another heavy chat, so I take my place on the opposite side of the sofa, setting my computer on my lap. Then I realize something. "Do you have WiFi?"

He looks up, but just briefly before returning to whatever it is he's working on. "Yup."

I shake my head. "I really wish I had thought of that earlier. I could have FaceTimed using that."

He frowns. "Sorry. I hadn't thought of it either. Yes, I guess you could have."

I make a mental note to call Rina tonight using that, and then I open my laptop, log on and open a brand-new Word document page. My eyes drift out the window and then over to Miles who sits across from me, his back against the cushioned arm as he faces me, sketching away. I mirror his position, our feet about a foot or so apart.

Pulling the blanket over my legs, I offer him some. "I share."

He grins, his hand moving a mile a minute. He reaches around his legs and takes some of the blanket, covering his socked feet, and then goes right back to work. I take the hint and do the same as images and words springboard to the front of my mind, my fingers taking over, typing away as words turn into sentences, turn into paragraphs and scenes.

I pick a little at the food, sipping on my wine while Miles drinks his beer, both of us lost in our work as the fire crackles and Betsy works on her bone, having decided to join us out here with it now that it's warm.

Some untold time later, I move for the first time in what feels like hours, my back stiff and my ass aching. I realize I banged out well over two thousand words and though I haven't read back through any of it, I already know I'm going to like it. But between the wine and the fire and the snow outside, my head grows heavy.

Shutting my laptop, I set it down on the coffee table, scooting myself down some and staring out at the snow. It looks like hell out there, but I'm in heaven here, warm and comfortable and… really happy.

Miles's hand on my feet startles me and my head jolts over, catching his eyes and his smirk. He tugs them gently toward him, allowing me to stretch out beside him, and his hand starts to work, rubbing in the arch of my feet.

"Stop being so perfect," I tell him on a yawn, my eyes closing on their own volition.

"You first," I think I hear him whisper just as I start to doze. Wondering if I'll have another steamy dream featuring my very own Superhero Miles.

Chapter Eleven

MILES

I watch as London's breathing evens out and once I know she's good and asleep, I release her foot and return to my sketches. Something I haven't done in a while but am really enjoying. At first, I started with different objects I've always wanted to make. A chandelier I've had in my head for a while, but never started on. Some wine and champagne glasses because those are huge sellers, especially in the wedding market. A few ornate objects that I think would be fun and challenging.

Then it happened.

Then I flipped a page and stared at the blank white in front of me.

London was still typing away, lost and deep in whatever world she was creating, and I didn't hesitate.

My hand started to move in a very old and familiar way, drawing the long lines and delicate slopes of her face and neck. The subtlety of the few freckles she has on the bridge of her adorable nose. The curve and swell of her heart-shaped lips that favor a hint of mischief and humor—especially with whatever she was writing. The arch of her eyes, bright and alive against the fan of her long, dark lashes.

Her eyes. My favorite part of her for so much more than just the exotic color.

They're a book. An endless roadmap into London Canterbury's mind and heart and soul as she wears so much of that on her sleeve. Something I've always loved and admired. Something I've missed so goddamn much in the years I haven't been able to look into them.

I miss all the little things about her that I loved so much. Things I know I'm going to miss again once she leaves.

And my chest instantly hurts.

Watching as she sleeps so safe and comfortable beside me, I ache.

"This is why I kept my distance. Why I never engaged. Not only with you, but with everyone. With the world. I can't..." I sigh, that tightness in my chest growing, becoming more constricting. "I could so easily fall in love with you again, London. Easier than breathing. I don't want you to leave and it's only been one fucking day. How will I survive if I let you in fully only to watch you go the way everyone else in my life has?"

I stare down at the picture in my lap, at the perfect likeness I've drawn because I perfected it a long time ago.

That's when I feel it. The punch and the lack of wind in my lungs. My mind speeding up while simultaneously slowing down. The burn on my skin and the hum in my veins.

I never stopped loving her.

Not for a moment.

She's it. Always has been and I have a choice.

Enjoy her for as long as I have her and earn my pain when she goes.

Or resist her and die in a swell of regret because no matter what, the pain is coming for me.

I close up my sketchpad, setting it on the coffee table beside her laptop, placing my charcoal pencil on top. I look around the room, at the space we're in and though I want to carry her upstairs, this room is her heaven and I want to always remember her in it.

With me.

I take her feet back in my hands and I slide them over, moving her body until she's flat on her back. She stirs, but not much and I hesitate, wondering if I should be a gentleman and let her sleep instead of the beast who is gearing up to devour her whole.

As beautiful as she looks like this, I don't have the luxury of time to waste. She can sleep later; I'll make sure she's nice and tired when she falls asleep beside me tonight.

Sucking in a shuttering breath, I crawl up toward her, taking her hand and planting a kiss on the inside of her wrist. She smells like her body lotion and my dick stirs awake as my heart begins to gallop and my lips buzz with anticipation.

"Firefly," I whisper. I hadn't realized I said her nickname that night, but it doesn't surprise me either. Now the time for pretenses is gone. She knows my truth. Knows how much I want her. How much I've always wanted her. I slide up the thin material of her sweater and kiss the crook of her elbow. "Are you awake?"

Her breathing has changed so I know she is.

Her eyes flutter open, deep pools of purple that rob me of my senses as they grow darker before me.

"Tell me to stop if you don't want me to continue."

Her other hand reaches up and she drags her fingers through my hair to the back of my head. My eyes close at her touch, my skin snapping with heat and electricity and need. A craving so deep there is no sating it.

"Miles," she whispers my name in the softest of breaths and I reply by crashing my lips to hers, greedy as I hungrily take her for my own. She opens for me, deepening our exchange and I lower my body onto hers, shifting to remove some of my weight and kissing her with abandon.

Like the crazed, love-sick fool I am with her.

My hands cup her face, tilting her as I pepper her lips and cheeks with soft, sweet kisses before diving back in, my tongue stroking hers. Her hands grasp my shoulders, fisting at the cotton of my shirt as her teeth scrape my bottom lip. The groan on my lips turns into a growl as she starts to grind up against me, rubbing my rock-hard cock through my jeans and driving me insane.

I sit her up, my lips trailing down her jaw and neck, deep, open-mouthed, wet kisses that have her moaning, her head tilting back in pleasure. My hands sink beneath the hem of her sweater, caressing her warm, silky skin. But more importantly, giving her the choice to say no.

As if reading my thoughts, her chin drops, breaking our connection and smiling into my eyes. "Are we having a change of heart?"

I grin, leaning forward and rubbing my nose with hers, stealing a quick kiss because I don't know how to stop kissing her. Her mouth is my wonderland. "Definitely not."

"Then stop trying to be such a gentleman and dirty me up."

Holy shit. My cock just slammed against my zipper, begging for mercy and to grant it early parole.

Grasping the hem of her sweater, I rip it over her head, throwing it somewhere in the room. "You like it dirty, firefly. I can give it to you real dirty."

My mouth slams back down on hers, my hands fisting into her hair as I pull her closer to me. Grasping her ass, I haul her up as I shift my position, setting her back down on me so she's straddling my lap. We both hiss in pleasure at the contact, my hand sliding from her hair, along her neck, past her shoulder on down to her left breast where I cup it in my hand, testing its weight and squeezing.

I've had so many fantasies about this over the years. So many thoughts of how I would do this with her if ever given the chance. My thoughts an endless dirty buffet of possibilities.

I pull back to look down at her, staring at her tits, before gliding up every single inch, memorizing how she looks in this moment, her tits heaving with her pants and her body straddling mine. London glances down too for a flicker of a second before her eyes jolt up to mine. She smiles and something inside of me lights up in a way it never has before.

My thumb presses into her bottom lip, rubbing back and forth. "You're so beautiful, London. You have no idea how badly I want you."

And as I say the words, I know I mean them for so much more than sex.

For however long I can keep her, London Canterbury is mine.

My hands skim along her shoulders in feather-light kisses, my eyes on hers, watching as her breath speeds up and her eyes turn the color of midnight. I reach the clasp of her bra, unhooking it and letting the straps fall down to her upper arms. She sucks in a ragged breath as my mouth comes in, licking and nipping at her racing pulse while I slowly remove her bra.

The garment falls to the floor and my hands come up, cupping and squeezing her soft, insanely sexy tits in my large hands. I press them together, trussing them up as my head dips down, licking at one nipple then biting the other.

Not hard at first. Just a tease. Just something to rile her.

To get her grinding against me because she just can't fucking take the tension building inside her anymore.

She emits a breathy sigh followed by a whimper as my teeth scrape along her pebbled peak, sliding it back into my mouth and sucking on it while her head falls back, her hair tumbling down with it.

"Miles," she murmurs, her fingers diving into my hair, scraping along my scalp in a move that is so simple and yet so erotic, my dick pulses. I need more of her. I need to taste every inch. The way she says, "Oh god, yes," has me thinking I said that aloud.

Good.

My hands reach around her waist, twisting her body off mine and lowering her back down onto the couch. My mouth finds her neck, beginning a slow trail down, worshiping her perfect fucking breasts some more before licking the gorgeous underside of them. Her hands fly up, grabbing on to the arm of the sofa, giving me better access and Jesus Christ, I intend to take full advantage of that.

My fingers trail along her upper chest, following the path my mouth is creating as I go lower and lower, savoring every delicious inch of the goddess beneath me. I reach the button of her jeans and pop it with my teeth, lowering the zipper the same way since my hands are too busy on her body to bother with such a mundane task.

London is writhing, squirming around like she can't control herself.

My hands grasp her hips, pressing them down, stabilizing her before sliding down the denim of her jeans, past her hips and her pretty white panties, down her toned legs and onto the ground. London's skin is flushed, her breasts already red and marked from my hands and mouth, her neck too, and fuck...

"You are without a doubt, the sexiest fucking woman I've ever seen."

My hand rubs my cock over my jeans a couple of times as I take her in, feeling like a king when I haven't even begun to pleasure this woman the way I intend to. Her teeth hold her bottom lip captive, her eyes glued to mine, watching me as her chest rises and falls with the heavy lust swimming within her.

Skimming my nose up along her seam, through her panties, her back arches, a strained sound cutting out from her throat. She smells so good. So goddamn good I'm already losing my mind. I place a kiss along the smooth satin, right over her clit, before I slip the material to the side, taking in how gorgeous her wet pussy is before my tongue comes out, licking what I already know will be my favorite place in the world.

Inside London.

"Oh, hell," she gasps, her hands gripping the sofa as her eyes close and her head rocks back and to the side.

I remove her panties, my hands splaying on her inner thighs as I spread her apart. I dip my tongue in her again, thrusting in deeper this time, flicking it back and forth and loving the hell out of her muffled cries.

Sliding my tongue out, my thumb rubs along her clit as I lick her a little lower, testing her boundaries and grinning into her flesh when she jerks and then rolls her hips into my face. "You like that? Is this what you meant by dirty?"

"So good," she pants as I do it again, my thumb working her as my tongue fucks her pussy. "Oh god, that's so good."

"Mmmm," I hum into her, blowing cool air on her clit and driving her wild. "Such a sweet girl I'm gonna dirty up. Tell me, firefly. Tell me what you want. Do you want my tongue to fuck you, or my fingers? Do you want my mouth right here" —I flick her clit and she shudders, moaning louder with each go— "or my thumb?" I blow more cold air and her whole body starts to tremble, so close already.

"I-I. Fuck, Miles. Holy fuck."

"You have no idea how good I'm going to fuck you. How deep and hard. How full you'll be with my cock."

I roll her clit between my fingers, flicking it with my tongue and thrusting two fingers inside of her, pumping them as she starts to lose it. Her body convulses, her legs locking around my head as her hips shoot up, searching, begging as my tongue and fingers fuck her into a screaming frenzy.

I watch, enraptured by the way her body moves, how I'm the one doing this to her. It doesn't take a genius to know that I'm about as fucked as a man can get with a woman.

I never stood a chance.

Her body sags back down to the couch, her eyes closed and a smile taking over her whole face. She starts to laugh, reaching down blindly for my face. I help her out, loving the way she brushes the hair from my forehead and toys with the ends of my strands. I lick my lips, sliding my fingers out of her and licking those too. She sighs, that smile unshakable.

"That was so much better than any dream or even Christmas dinner."

I laugh, planting a soft kiss to her lower belly. "You're telling me."

She peeks one eye open, locking it with mine. "Now it's my turn."

Chapter Twelve

LONDON

One thing I did not expect? Miles's dirty mouth. And I'm not just talking about the magic of his wicked tongue, though that certainly deserves the Oscar for best performance. I mean, *damn*. I digress. What I didn't expect, other than that earth-shattering orgasm, was for him to be so vocal. For him to watch so closely.

It's hot. And sexy.

And I think I could seriously get off just from those two things alone.

Something I might have to try out in the form of naughty midnight phone sex if, *when*, I go.

But I don't want to think about that right now. No, in fact, all I want to do is focus on the sex on a stick man whose face is still between my legs, lips glistening with my orgasm, a dopey, pleased gleam in his eyes.

"What did you have in mind?" he asks, and I feel my eyebrows pinching in. He chuckles, kissing up my belly and taking a nipple in his mouth. "Did you forget already?"

"I think so because I have no idea what you're talking about. Blame it on the orgasm and the loss of brain cells."

He smiles against my skin, nipping at it playfully, but it feels so good and my mind starts to wander again, focusing on the things he does to me. "You said it was your turn."

Oh. I did, didn't I? Right. "I was thinking that I'd really like to hear how you sound when my mouth is on your dick."

Miles pauses, his dark eyes snapping up to mine before he groans. "Jesus, London. You say things like that, and I'll blow my load before you even get close to me with your mouth."

I grin mischievously. "Quick on the trigger?"

Now he growls, something low and animalistic. "Not even a little."

"We could have a race. First to make the other come wins. Or loses?" I tilt my head. "I'm not exactly sure how that one works out."

Miles laughs, kissing the dip at the base of my neck and scooping me up, cradling me into his arms as he brings me upright, back onto his lap. He kisses me, his tongue slipping into my mouth, taking possession of me in a way no one ever has before. I'm completely naked whereas Miles is still fully dressed. It feels weird, though I feel anything but self-conscious around this man.

Something about him makes me insanely comfortable. I can be me and he likes that, weird quirks and silliness and all.

But still, the clothes have to go.

Without breaking the kiss, I go for the hem of his shirt, tugging it up. Miles picks up on my intention, reaching one hand behind his head, grasping the material of his shirt and helping me along as we slip it over his head.

And much the way he did with me, I pull back, taking in everything that is Miles.

His broad, muscular shoulders, the thick bulge of his biceps as they flex beneath my touch. My hands don't linger there long, too anxious to continue their exploration. His chest has a light dusting of hair on his pecs and I drag my nail through it, loving the sensation as it coasts along my fingertips.

His abs, much like the rest of him, are all muscles, hard lines, and sharp ridges. I find another sexy patch of hair below his navel and I follow it down until it disappears into the hem of his boxers and jeans.

Miles hasn't stopped touching me.

His fingers caress my back, up and down, mapping out every dip and curve of my body, tracking his touch with his eyes that have difficulty staying in one place. He likes to look at my face, I realize. Likes to stare into my eyes and watch the way his touch affects me.

A girl really could get used to having such an attentive and focused lover.

I start to slide off his lap, my knees going to the floor and just as I land, already a little uncomfortable, Miles jerks me back up with a shake of his head. "As much as I'm dying for you to be on your knees in front of me with my cock in your mouth, I'm not letting you do that with your knee the way it is."

"But—"

"Nope. We can play around with that later. In my bed. But right now" —his hand cups my face, his eyes always on mine— "I really want to be inside of you, London. Only…" He trails off and I already know what he's going to say.

Condoms.

"I haven't been with anyone in months, and I was tested after the last time. I'm clean and I have an IUD."

Miles grins, bringing my face back in to kiss me. "Are you sure? I'm clean too. It's been a while for me and like you said, I've been tested. But I've never done it without a condom. I just want you to be sure."

I know what he's saying. "I've never done it without a condom either," I tell him, matching his tone. It's more than the trust behind it. It's the notion that it's just him and me, no barrier.

He blows out a shaky breath and I take advantage, my mouth claiming his once more.

"God, this is going to hurt," he murmurs, almost to himself. In fact, it takes me a moment to fully grasp what he's saying. And when I do, my heart aches in a way it never has before.

Raising up on my knees, I reach down between us, unbuttoning his jeans and drawing down his zipper. A howl of wind rushes past the house, rattling the windows and causing the fire in the fireplace to sway as some of it seeps down the chimney.

Outside the storm is raging while in here, ours is just getting started.

Miles helps me out, lifting up and sliding his jeans and boxer briefs down, kicking them off. I grasp his cock in my hand, loving the grunt from Miles as I do. He's so perfect. So hard and long and thick. He's going to feel so good; I already know it.

Miles clasps my hips, guiding me as I angle my body, moving his cock into me. Inch by inch, I slide down on him until he's fully seated inside of me, filling me up so full I can hardly stand it.

His forehead drops to mine, a bead of sweat already forming on his temple. "London," he rasps. My heart thunders. My body buzzes. *This* is what my body is saying. *This is how it's always meant to feel. This is who you were always meant to have inside of you.*

"Miles," I whisper back, equally as softly, full of just as much emotion and wonder because as much as I'm feeling this, I know he is too.

I rock forward and his eyes slam shut. I do it again, my hips undulating, my body playing with him, driving him crazy. It feels good, but it's not enough. He wants me to move. He wants me to bounce.

But watching this strong, gorgeous man lose his mind in my body is something else.

After a few minutes of this, he growls, his teeth meeting my shoulder, biting at my flesh and I throw my head back and let my body take over. I rise up and slam down on him, unexpectedly crying out his name, almost in surprise. His mouth consumes my breasts and throat as his hips thrust up, his hands on my ass guiding me along.

What started out as a tease has turned into something primal. Something driven by need and instinct. Two bodies coming together as one. Skin against skin as pleasure builds within me. He fucks me like this, hard and unrelenting, grunting and groaning into me.

"You're so fucking tight." *Thrust.* "Jesus, London." *Thrust.* "The way your pussy squeezes my cock." *Thrust.* "Over and over again." *Thrust.* "I can't get enough." *Thrust.* "I don't want to stop."

"Don't stop," I moan. "Please, Miles."

Miles lifts me off of him, spinning me around and then slamming me back down, impaling me at a new angle. I cry out, his cock hitting the most perfect fucking spot in the history of perfect spots this way. My head falls back against his shoulder and his mouth consumes mine, ravaging me as he continues to fuck me relentlessly.

We're all tongues and teeth and lips. I can't get close enough. My hands reach behind me, grasping the back of his head, holding him closer as my breathing becomes too ragged to continue kissing.

"Come, firefly. I want your pretty pussy to come all over my cock. My hot cum to fill you up."

Holy mother of god, I'm about to lose my mind.

He spreads my legs, throwing my knees on either side of his, and the moment his fingers find my clit and start to rub me, I detonate.

My body explodes, shattering into pieces of light and sound and space.

He continues to pound into me, harder, his movements jerky as he too reaches his climax. He bellows out a roar, cursing, his face planting into the dip between my neck and shoulder as he stills and shakes, giving me everything he has before sagging back into the sofa.

I sag with him, my body rising and falling with his heavy uneven breaths as I try to catch my own.

Miles folds my arms across my belly, wrapping his own around them, holding me against him so tight my eyes start to burn with tears.

Miles.

A broken prince with the heart of a lion. If I didn't believe in true love or fate before, here, in his arms, I certainly do now. And I don't know how I'll be able to leave that behind.

Chapter Thirteen

MILES

London ends up falling asleep in my arms. I hadn't realized at first. I cleaned her up and we both got dressed. But the second all that was done, I snatched her back. Holding her, unable to let her go, needing her against me, with me, for as long as I could selfishly manage it.

And my girl fell asleep.

Lifting her up into my arms, I cradle her against me as I carry her through my house. I could just let her sleep out here on the sofa, but it's getting late and the fire is dwindling, and we turned off the space heater. So instead I walk her up the stairs, kissing her forehead and unsure where to take her.

I want to take her into my room. I want to put her down on my bed. I want to tuck her in under my blankets. But I also don't want to presume or push her or whatever the fuck goes through girls' minds.

I'm not good with this stuff. Never have been.

Loving someone has only led to pain, and though I know that's ultimately where this is headed, I don't want her to know how far gone I already am, have always been, with her. It'll scare her, and I can't have that.

I'm on borrowed time as it is.

Decision made, I bring her back to the bedroom she slept in last night, setting her down and kissing her lips as I tuck her in. "I'm going to be outside, clearing out some of the snow so it's easier to manage tomorrow or the next day. Okay?" I ask. She moans softly, rolling over. "I'm only putting you in here because it felt like the right thing to do by you, but tonight, I want you to sleep in my room with me."

She doesn't make a sound to this, so I kiss her forehead again and leave.

Betsy greets me at the garage door, already knowing my intention as I climb into all my winter gear. I step out into the three-bay garage and glance over quickly at London's Porsche. It has a nice dent in the front on the driver's side, and I'm curious why the airbags didn't deploy. That's likely why she hurt her head.

She won't be able to drive it up to her parents' house, and the thought of her driving herself in a rental car makes me sick. I could let her take my SUV, but the truth is, I want to take her. Make sure she gets to her family safely, but then what? Do I just turn around and leave her there?

The thought of leaving her twists like a knife in my gut. Though I knew better before I ever touched her, the thought of losing her already hurts so much more than anything else has before. Because even if she asks me to stay, she'll eventually return home and I'll do the same.

The garage doors are not powered by the generator, so I tug on the emergency open cord, hoisting it up and pulling the door open. Betsy goes flying out into the show, the way she always does, and I wheel the huge snowblower I have out, cranking it up with a deafening roar.

I push thoughts of London leaving out of my head.

I learned long ago that I can't control the things others do. I can only control my reaction to them. I didn't fight for London the first time. I never thought I was entitled to. But if I let that woman walk out of my life without a fight this time, I'll regret it for the rest of my life and I already have enough of those.

Tucking the hood of my coat down lower over my beanie, I push the machine out into the deep, heavy snow. It's coming down harder now than it was even last night and it's not supposed to let up until tomorrow afternoon.

By then, we could easily have more than three feet of snow.

I plow out my driveway and the long walkway that leads from the street up to my front porch. By the time I wheel the snowblower back inside the garage, corral Betsy in, and step back into the house, I'm a nasty mess, reeking of gasoline.

I dry Betsy off with a towel I leave back here for her and stomp off the excess snow on the mudroom floor. After hanging everything up, I head into the main part of the house only to stop dead at the vision before me. London is wearing a green sweater and flannel pants, her long hair twisted up on top of her head in some kind of bun. She's moving about my kitchen, making herself at home - as she cooks, listening to Christmas music as it pipes in from the speaker on her phone.

"Hey," she exclaims, a radiant smile lighting up her face. "I figured since you've been doing all the cooking and snow plowing, I should make us some dinner."

I stare unmoved, blinking like a mindless fool.

She tilts her head, some of that smile slipping. "Is that okay? I hope you don't mind that I sort of went through your kitchen a little."

I can only shake my head.

"Right. Well, I know how to make three things and lucky for me, you have the ingredients to make one of them."

"What three things?"

"Burritos, veggie stir-fry, and chicken parm with homemade sauce. In case you're curious, we're eating the latter."

"Okay."

She walks over to me, running her hands up my chest until they're locked around my neck. "Are you?"

Am I?

"Yes. I've never been better."

It's the absolute truth and when she reads that in my eyes, she climbs up on her tiptoes and kisses me. She tastes spicy like the sauce she's making and sweet like the wine she's drinking and I'm so high on London Canterbury that there is no coming down.

The heart wants what it wants, and mine has never stopped wanting her.

All too soon she pulls back, crinkling her nose. "Go shower, Miles. You smell like gasoline. Then come back down and kiss me some more and then we'll make the chicken and garlic bread together."

"Yes ma'am."

She steps back and I turn to do as instructed when I feel a sharp swat on my ass. I spin back around, my eyes wide as a shocked smile hits me square in the face.

"There it is. Much better. You were getting too serious. And just so you're not confused, I took what you said to heart when you tucked me into bed earlier and I moved some of my sleeping stuff into your room. I'm judging based on the lube and iPad on your nightstand that you take the side closest to the bathroom, so I went for the other side."

An embarrassed laugh tumbles out of me, but all London does is wink and then skip back into the kitchen.

"Get a move on, Superhero Miles. I'm getting hungry and this dinner won't make itself."

I watch a moment as London kneels down to Betsy, who is barking unhappily at the music. I listen as she tells her that Christmas music is life this time of year, but to make her happy, she'll put on a Christmas song by Taylor Swift. She does just that and then she gives her a treat from my cabinet, rubbing behind her ears just the way Betsy likes.

I watch London in my home, overwhelmed with the certainty that there is nowhere else she's meant to be.

Now I just have to get her to agree with me.

Chapter Fourteen

LONDON

I listen as Miles takes the stairs two at a time. His door closes and then the sound of water running through pipes accompanies the music streaming from my phone. My body is jittery and my mind restless. And as if the universe knows I'm a hot second from going postal and hacking his upstairs bathroom door down with an ax and saying, 'Here's London,' the music on my phone cuts out and my FaceTime lights up with Rina's number.

I dive for it, far less graceful than I should be with a bum knee. My hands grasp my phone, grappling with it as it nearly falls out of my hands and onto the floor. I catch it, hitting accept and staring straight into my friend's annoyed face.

She blinks at me with wide, pale blue eyes. "You're not missing. Savannah called me yesterday and said she couldn't make it for New Year's because you're missing."

I roll my eyes. "Why do you ever listen to either of my sisters?"

"Because she's an attending in my hospital. Well." She shrugs. "Former hospital."

"You can't really move to Boston."

She sighs. We've had this chat before. "It's done kittle lips.

Boston, you're my home," she sings. "Cue all the dun-duns that go in that song. Where are you if you're not missing?"

I look over my shoulder and when I find that the coast is clear, I say, "I had a small accident."

Rina's eyebrows pinch together as she blows some of her long bangs out of her face. "And are you trapped in a hole by the lotion in a basket dude from *Silence of the Lambs*?"

"No. Why would you ask that?"

"Because you're being cryptic as hell and looking over your shoulder, London. Because your sister called me yesterday and asked if I knew where you were because you never made it to your parents' house."

"I'm fine. I spoke to my father last night."

"Well, great. No one thought to message me about it. I called your phone like a bazillion times and it went straight to voicemail."

"Yeah. I have no cell service here."

Rina growls under her breath, obviously already at her end with me. "I know. You freaking emailed me earlier, remember? And all you said in your email is that you need me to FaceTime you so you can use the WiFi since you have no cell coverage. So, what the fuck, London?!" she yells. "You seriously had me worried out of my mind after those calls yesterday, but now that I see you, you're smiling and a bit flushed, so dish it, sister."

"I crashed into a tree and hit my head and my knee. I was saved by a passing motorist who happened to be a guy I went to high school with… aa guy I always secretly had a crush on who apparently always secretly had a crush on me back."

Rina's eyes are comically wide. "You're kidding me."

I shake my head, shrugging sheepishly though I don't know why I feel strange saying this. Maybe because that crush turned into a whole hell of a lot more this afternoon. "No. Weird coinkidink, right?"

She snorts. "That's one word for it. But you're really okay?"

"I'm great."

"Oh snap." She points at me through the phone. "You're blushing like a virgin on prom night after the dance is over."

"I am not," I clip indignantly when I know it's a lie and so does Rina.

"Girl, we *soooo* need to talk about this. I want to hear all about mister crush and…" Her eyes pop open wider if that's even possible. "Well hello there, sexy sir. And who might you be?"

"Huh?" I push out until I catch a glimpse of Miles in the reflected image in the corner of the screen.

"Mister crush? Sexy sir?"

My eyes slam shut. "Too late to hide now, London. He heard you."

"Thanks," I mutter dryly. "I missed that somehow."

Miles chuckles behind me, coming in close and wrapping his hand around my waist. "I'm Miles, actually."

"Rina. Thank you for saving my girl."

I open my eyes millimeter by millimeter and see Miles's amused grin behind me.

"Any time." He comes in close to my ear and whispers, "Every time. Crush, huh?"

I roll my shoulder, brushing him away. "I was just being polite. I thought it rude to tell Rina I can't stand you after you saved me."

He pinches my side, kisses my cheek, and laughs at my expression. "Nice to meet you, Rina." He throws her a wave before going to fix Betsy some food.

Rina's jaw is now somewhere on the ground. "Um. Wow. Yeah, okay then. You're going to call me again. Soon. And we'll talk when Mister Sexy Crush can't hear us."

"I thought it was Mister Crush and Sexy Sir," he yells out, and I flip him off, making him laugh once more at my expense.

She shakes her head. "I've shortened it, but the name definitely still fits," she replies in an equally loud voice. She winks at me, her tone dropping. "Be safe. Use condoms."

"Rina!"

She laughs. "Seriously, love you. Call me soon."

"Love you, too."

I disconnect the call and turn to find Miles standing on the opposite side of the kitchen, smirking at me. "You're blushing."

Rina said the same damn thing. How red am I? "And you look pretty smug."

He hitches up a shoulder. "Your friend seems nice."

"You're just saying that because you like the nickname she gave you."

He shoves away from the counter, purpose in his stride. The look in his eyes has my pulse racing. "Can't blame a guy for that. It's a great nickname."

"If not a bit inaccurate," I manage, my voice coming out husky.

"Oh." He tilts his head, not buying my bullshit for a second. He draws closer and instinctively, I back up until I bump into the counter. "So, you don't think I'm sexy?" he questions, that delicious smirk still deviously attached to his lips.

"I guess you're alright. If you're into the thick hair, blue eyes, dimples, muscular thing."

"And you're not?"

I shake my head, biting into my lip and curling my toes in my socks because the tension is killing me. I want to run, and I want to jump him while wrapping my legs around his waist. The man is seriously killing me with his panty-melting—and wetting—looks and slow, sexy drawl.

He reaches me, standing directly in front of me without touching. I have to crane my neck to meet his eyes. He's wearing his glasses now and damn; I really love the way he looks in those.

His face dips, his mouth skimming along my cheek toward my ear, his hot breath on my skin sending chills up my spine. "What about the crush part?" he hums into me and my freaking eyes roll back in my head. Jesus. This man and that voice and his scent and did I mention, *Jesus*?

"You first," I say because I'm kinda a wimp right now. He already heard me, which means he already knows the answer and is enjoying the hell out of playing with me. Fine. I like being played with, so he's lucky in that, but a little positive reinforcement goes a long way too.

His nose skims along the shell of my ear before trailing south. He plants a kiss right below my ear and my knees start to buckle. I feel his smile against my skin as his arm snakes around my back, steadying me.

"You want to know if I have a crush on you back?"

He plants another kiss and my hands fly up, clutching on to his shoulders, my nails digging in as he tortures me with his lips and tongue. I can't speak, so I just nod.

"London Amelia Canterbury, I cannot remember a time when I didn't have a crush on you. In fact, the term *crush* is woefully inadequate. I moved way past that back in high school."

Damn. That's it.

It's official.

My heart just spring-boarded out of my chest and landed in his. And the strangest part of all, it doesn't feel weird or too soon. It feels like years in the making. Like all that time in between then and now was just a buildup to this.

Without a second thought, I push him away. His face morphs instantly into one of hurt and surprise, but he'll get over it. Hoisting myself up onto the counter, I grab the back of his head and drag him into me, kissing him like I have never kissed a man before. A groan slips past his throat and I greedily swallow it down, loving the way his desperation tastes on my tongue.

My legs intertwine behind his back and I pull him in even closer, pressing our bodies together so there is no separation between us.

His mouth glides down my neck as my fingers fist his hair. "London," he growls against me. "How are you getting up to your parents'?"

"Huh?" I drag him off me, staring into his eyes.

"Buzz kill?"

I laugh. "A bit. You mentioned my parents while kissing me. But why did you ask?"

"Because your car is dented and unsafe to drive. And…" He swallows, his eyes on mine, suddenly hard as stone, but I don't miss the uncertainty dancing in the background. "I'd like to drive you up."

"You would?"

"Yeah. Would that be okay?"

Now it's my turn to swallow. Putting yourself out there emotion-ally is tricky business. "Would you stay with us for Christmas?"

He puffs out a breath, running a hand through his hair. I feel him trying to pull away, but uh-uh, he's not going anywhere.

"Christmas is hard for me."

Shit. I can only imagine it is. "Will you think about it? I'd like you to. If that counts for anything," I tack on.

"It counts for everything, it's just…"

"What? Tell me, Miles."

His mouth reclaims mine, and I hold him against me, hugging him while he kisses me. Letting him know he can trust me. Telling him without words that I'm already in so deep with him that the idea of him dropping me off and then leaving scares the crap out of me.

"I'll think about it," he whispers against my lips, but I feel hesi-tation now in his touch. He's putting up walls that I want to knock down, but don't know how. Partially because I understand his reservation.

Maybe asking him to stay is stupid.

The longer this goes on, the more time I'm with him, the more I want this man. I'm not sure there is a limit to how much. I want to learn him. Study up on all things Miles. Swim freely and openly in the ocean that are his eyes.

But underneath it all is a searing, ugly reality: Sooner or later we will have to part.

Chapter Fifteen

MILES

Life is short. That's what keeps echoing through my head as I finish up the dishes as London puts away the leftovers. We didn't have sex on my kitchen counter the way I had wanted to. Obviously my big mouth got in the way of that, but the truth is, cooking dinner and eating it was a nice distraction from the brewing maelstrom in my head.

My sole purpose for wanting to drive London north to her parents' is to spend as much time with her as I can before saying goodbye. Knowing goodbye is imminent and resigned to making the most of the time I have with her before that happens. Then she threw the curveball of asking me to join her and her family for Christmas.

I know how important Christmas with her family is to her. I told her my hang-ups with the fucking miserable holiday I'd just as quickly forget exists.

The problem is, she's likely here through Christmas Eve and if I can get her up to her parents' by noon on Christmas Day, it'll be a miracle.

But that doesn't change the invitation.

An invitation I'm both dying to accept and decline in the same breath.

I don't want to let London go. But all that time I was upstairs in the shower, I realized one very significant thing.

I can't ask her to stay.

She lives in New York. She has a life there. An apartment. And she's literally only been in my home for a little more than a day.

If I tell her where my feelings lie, she'll likely laugh at me.

Or just smile and nod and say something witty because she's too sweet to laugh at me. But it's not like I can actually ask her to stay. Ask her to move here and be with me. She'll say no, and I wouldn't blame her for that.

In a perfect world, in another life, London and I are the stuff of happily ever afters.

Just not in this one.

It's a sobering truth that has my stomach twisting as we finish up in the kitchen and the 'what next' starts to loom heavily over us. But it also solidifies my plans for the next however long I have with her.

Everything else I'll weather after. I won't have a choice.

"Did you want to watch that movie you mentioned last night?"

Her head whips around at light speed, her eyes wide like she was so lost in her own introspection that she forgot I was here. "Yes," she says quickly. Too quickly. "Have you seen it?"

"*Christmas Vacation?*" I smile stupidly at her concerned frown. "I think everyone has at some point, right? I watched some of that *A Christmas Story* marathon last year."

"I love that one too. *Love Actually* is another one of my favs."

"Nope. Sorry. That sounds like a chick flick."

She frowns and it's sexy and adorable. "It's the best chick flick though. Does that count?" I shake my head. "Not even for a blowjob?"

Shit. She did not just go there with that.

"Keep talking." I take a step toward her because now there is a distinct hunger in her eyes that calls to every fucking cell in my body. It also drives all my available blood flow south and my ability to reason or object goes with it.

Girl licks her lips like she knows—she definitely knows—it's the nail in my coffin. Or bulge in my boxers at this point.

"I was thinking that maybe, since I haven't seen that one in a really long time and it's one of my *favorites*," she emphasizes, batting her long eyelashes at me like I'm a mindless fool who will fall for that—newsflash: I am, "that we could watch that together while I suck your cock until you come down my throat."

Shit.

"You really do not fight fair."

She shakes her head, a smile she's fighting and failing to hide crawling up her lips. "Nope. Not when it comes to the things I want."

I reach for her, cupping her face in my hand and tilting it, exposing her neck for me. "And right now, you want my cock in your mouth while you watch a chick flick?"

"Without a doubt," she murmurs as my lips meet her pulse. I lick it, from the base of her neck up to her jaw.

"How's this then, go put it on. I have every freaking paid streaming service there is. Do that for me and I'll think about letting you suck my cock."

She squirms and I'm so gone on her that there is no way any other woman in the history of the world stands a chance.

I trail back up, kissing her lips and spinning her around, pushing her in the direction of the living room and the television with a swat to her sensational ass. I adjust my bulge as I watch her go, catching the coy eye she throws over her shoulder in my direction.

What the hell am I going to do when she's gone?

Shrivel up and die, my brain chimes in and I mentally give myself the finger.

I toss Betsy a new bone because she goes through them like M&M's and then I make my way over to London, who is now sitting comfortably on my sofa, the movie queued up on the screen with some dude and some chick standing awkwardly waving while confetti rains down around them.

"Tell me about this movie." I press play on the remote, sitting down beside her, and the second I turn away from the television to her, she looks worried. "What?"

"The mother is dead in this."

"Huh?"

She clears her throat. "I just remembered. There is this little boy who is living with his stepdad because his mother just died."

"And you think almost twenty years later, I'm going to crumble like a gingerbread cookie and fall apart over that?"

She blows out a breath. "I'm just mentioning it."

I lean in and kiss her sweet, far too considerate mouth. "I'm fine, London. A full grown-up and everything. Besides, my mom didn't die. The bitch is still out there somewhere."

Evidently that's the wrong thing to say because London's eyes grow glassy and she looks at me like she wants to fix all my broken pieces. She doesn't yet understand that I don't need her to fix me; I just need her. Period. The end.

"How's this, firefly," I whisper, kissing the corner of her frown. "I splay you out, lick your pussy until you come on my face while you suck my cock, but we angle you so you can watch your film all the while?"

"A dirty sixty-nine while watching a chick flick?"

"Sound good?"

"Sounds great. That seriously might just be one of my filthy fantasies come true."

I cock an eyebrow. "Now you're just messing with me."

"Kinda but not really. I honestly have never envisioned such a scenario, but now that I am, I'm on board."

My mouth possesses hers in a rough kiss that has her panting by the time I pull away. "Stand up," I command, and she instantly obeys. It makes me insanely hard. Everything about London has me yearning.

"You're very bossy," she comments, and I laugh.

"Do you not like it?"

"I love it. I'm just… a little surprised, I guess."

"When you knew me as a teenager, I always felt out of control with everything. Now as a man, I thrive on it. Especially with this." I run my hand across her belly. "Pull off your sweater and then remove your pants."

She emits a shaky breath and then quickly gets to work on her clothes. Then she's standing before me in nothing but her panties while the television spews some stuff in British accents. Her head turns in that direction and my hands clasp her hips, my fingers on her ass cheeks as I guide her forward, my nose pressing in on her pussy and inhaling deeply.

My mouth pools and my cock thickens as I slide her panties down until they're on the floor. My tongue comes out, taking a taste that has her moaning, her hands fisting my hair as she rocks into my face.

"Take your bra off and lie down for me, legs spread."

"If I didn't explain this just now, I really like this side of you. The sexy, controlling, dirty talking one."

I look up into her soft, playful smile and kiss her belly. "If I didn't tell you this earlier, I really like everything about you, London."

Her smile grows, her eyes sparkling as she leans down and kisses me. Not in a frenzied, we're about to get it on way. But in a deep, passionate, and intense way that tells me I'm not alone in this. That maybe, somehow, there could be more for us.

With my hands on her ass, I shift until I'm on my back and bring her pussy over my face. She tries to move, tries to angle herself so she can complete the dirty sixty-nine we just talked about, but if her mouth even comes anywhere near my cock, I'll lose focus, and right now, I want to make my girl come.

"Miles," she gasps as my tongue starts to flick her clit, sucking it into my mouth and sliding two fingers inside her. She's soaked, already dripping down my hand. I growl into her, unable to hold it back. My fingers pump into her, picking up speed as my tongue licks her.

But my girl is undeterred.

Just as eager and hungry for me as I am for her.

She climbs off me, despite my protests and attempts to stop her. She gives me a wicked grin, the devil burning up her eyes. My hand trails along her thigh, squeezing her ass as she climbs back on me, sitting on my face from behind.

There is nothing sexier than a woman who is comfortable with herself. With her body. With her sexuality.

London is all of those things.

It makes me want to give her every ounce of pleasure she's craving.

London undoes the button and zipper on my pants and just as an insanely annoying drum starts to pound on the television and she giggles, her lips wrap around my cock, sucking it hard and deep into her mouth.

"Holy fuck," I hiss, stars dancing behind my eyes. "Don't you have a gag reflex? Jesus, London."

She laughs some more, the vibrations shooting up my balls and through my stomach, and I can easily say this is, without a doubt, the best day of my life.

I continue to feast on London's pussy, licking and touching every inch of her I can. But, as I knew would happen, my mind is clouding over in my own lust. Her fist is around the base of my dick, twisting and jerking it as she takes me in, bobbing up and down, slurping me up like a fucking champ.

It's mind-blowing.

It's erotic.

It's absolutely killing me.

My thumb rubs the ring of her opening, pressing in, but not going deeper as my teeth gently graze her clit. Something about that has her moaning louder, has her writhing and grinding against my lips and chin. I do it again, pressing back toward her ass with my thumb inside of her and she goes crazy.

Her hips are all over the place like she can't control them. Her mouth deepens its pull, bottoming out close to the base of my cock as she finally makes a gagging sound. And shit. Her gagging on my cock with her pussy grinding on my face. It's everything.

"London," I growl. "I'm gonna—"

She jerks me harder, not letting me free from her mouth.

She wants it.

She wants all of me as she hollows her cheeks, gagging some more while saliva drips down over her hand that's around me. I take her clit in my mouth and suck on it, flicking it with my tongue and fucking her with my thumb.

She explodes in a gush of wetness that coats my lips and tongue. She screams, her free hand gripping my thigh, her nails digging in and I lose it. I come hard and loud, shooting into her mouth and down her throat, fireworks detonating with the power of grenades behind my eyes.

London gives me one long last pull before releasing me. Her body is still poised over my face and I kiss her. Her opening. Her ass cheeks.

She spins back around, crawling up my chest and settling in. I lean in, kissing her lips, both of us tasting ourselves on the other. Her eyes are sleepy, and her smile is happy as I hold her against me, the television still playing one of her favorite Christmas movies.

I grab the throw blanket from the end of the sofa and wrap us up in it, kissing her temple while she watches her movie and I watch her.

I'm so in love with everything about this woman.

A woman I never got over. A woman I could spend my life worshiping. A woman I want to shower with everything that she deserves.

A woman I want to beg to stay but can't force the words out.

Chapter Sixteen

LONDON

When I open my eyes and take in the fucking snow that's still falling from the heavens, I frown.

It's Christmas Eve today.

And typically, if this were any other Christmas Eve, I'd wake up to breakfast with my family. We'd all sit around the dining room table, eating a buffet of food our chef cooks up for us while drinking coffee, telling stories, and teasing the hell out of each other. In the town I grew up in, my family was something of a rarity. And not because of our money because that was as ubiquitous as water is in the ocean there.

No, it's because we didn't have drama.

No messy divorces or parents hating each other. My father didn't screw around on our mother and marry his twenty-one-year-old assistant. My sisters and I were raised to never bully, to be kind and generous, and treat others as you'd want them to treat you.

It wasn't just lip service with them either.

My parents led by example, treating everyone with dignity and respect, regardless of socioeconomic status, race, gender, sexual orientation, whatever. To my parents, having money didn't make them better than anyone else. It's why when Miles said I was nice to everyone, I felt a surge of pride.

Which is why this year above all others is the hardest not to be with them.

So while many of my old friends are busy avoiding their families for the holidays, choosing to escape to Aspen or the Caribbean, I'm desperate to be with mine.

And I want Miles to be there with me.

Miles and I snuggled for the remainder of the film. He watched it with me, holding me close and tickling my bare skin throughout like he couldn't stop touching me. Sort of like what he's doing now as his fingers drag along the curve and dip from my ribs down to my hipbone.

He hasn't spoken yet and it doesn't take a genius to figure out he's got a lot on his mind.

The last thing in the world I want to do is guilt him. He needs to make this decision on his own. Telling him how badly I want him there will bring out the hero in him and I can't have that. I have no idea what this is between us. It came on strong and fast, much like the storm that's still whipping up a flurry of shit outside the window.

But that doesn't make it any less real.

As I said, this was more a long time coming than anything else.

Finally, I feel his mouth meet the crook of my neck and I know, I just freaking know, that whatever all that's sitting in his mind or on his shoulders is why it took him so long to do so.

But really, at the end of the day, what am I pushing for? Would I consider moving up here? Would he even want that? I mean, talk about moving quickly—pun intended. That's lunacy.

Even if I can envision it.

"Are you hungry?" he grumbles against me, his scruffy beard the best tickle on the planet.

"Starving."

"You never asked how I know how you take your coffee."

My eyes pop open wide, staring unseeing before me. "I hadn't thought about it."

I feel his smile against me, the bridge of his nose rubbing against my shoulder. "I used to do my own grocery shopping. The place where I lived, well, it was more like a boarding house than a home. Each kid, and there were three others like me, all had to do their own cooking and things. Coffee has always been my vice and I couldn't exactly afford eight dollars a day on Starbucks."

"I hate Starbucks. I know that's like sacrilegious and whatever, but it always tasted bitter to me."

"Yeah, that is sacrilegious."

I laugh, bumping my ass back into him and his smile grows, kissing my shoulder blade.

"Your family chef and the grounds guy…"

"Conrad," I fill in for him.

"Conrad. Cool guy. Anyway, the two of them would hit the supermarket on Sundays and that was usually my day too. I saw them there once and overheard them mention your name. Not a lot of London's out there, so I knew it was you. I stood in the aisle, like a weird creeper, reading the label of something I don't remember and listening to your family chef laugh about how you like half and half and enough sugar to—"

"Give a walrus cavities," I finish, and he chuckles.

"Yep. That's what she said."

I groan. "She's been saying that since I started drinking coffee freshman year. I like it pale and sweet."

"Like your skin," he hums into me, kissing me some more.

"I can't believe you remember that all these years later."

"I remember everything about you, London. You were my obsession. My greatest desire. The queen of all my dreams and biggest fantasies."

"That makes me angry."

He nips at my shoulder. "Me too. But I was a scared kid and there was no getting around the differences between you and me back then."

Maybe not. Still, I never saw those differences. Though that's likely naïve on my part.

"I like that you know how I take my coffee." My eyes close,

cinching just a little tight. I'm not used to giving so much of myself up to a man and yet with Miles, I can't seem to stop.

"I do too. But I don't know how you got your name. Like I said, not a lot of London's walking around."

"You ready to be grossed out?"

"Um. I don't know how to answer that."

I smile. "I'm London. My sisters are Savannah and Charleston. Each named after the place we were conceived."

"You're joking."

"Nope. I wish. How weird is that to tell people when they ask why my name is London?"

"Kind of weird. Better Pittsburg or something."

I laugh, nodding in agreement.

"I'm glad I know," he says softly.

"Me too. You know a lot about me now."

"I like that I know you prefer bacon over sausage. I like that I know you drown your pancakes in syrup. I like that today is the start of your favorite holiday, and I hate that I can't get you up to be with your family on it."

That makes two of us.

I roll over in his arms, kissing his prickly jaw and pushing thoughts of Christmas Eve with my family out of my mind. It doesn't help to dwell on things I can't change. That shit just drives you mad. All you can do is face another day and take it as it comes.

I'm learning that.

The hard way.

"What's on tap for today?"

His face buries into the crook of my shoulder, kissing a sweet trail that sends sparks of fire through my body, straight down to my core. "After I'm done making you scream my name, I thought I'd make breakfast. Then I have some things I need to work on in my shop."

"That's fine," I tell him because he sounds a bit nervous as he says that last part, though I don't know why. I'm the interloper in his house. "I have work I need to do myself."

And that's when his mouth covers mine. That's when he tells me every dirty thought and fantasy that floats through his head. That's when he slowly rises up, pressing all his weight into his hands, staring straight into my eyes, and sliding inside my body.

I surrender to him. I'm not sure I have any choice in the matter.

I could fool myself and spew things out like it's just sex or a connected history or despair over not being with my family for the holiday we all look forward to spending together.

But it would be a lie.

This thing goes deeper than that, and as his hand holds my face steady and his eyes pierce mine and his body claims what's left of me, I know the truth. And I do nothing to hide it from him. Let him make of that as he will.

Chapter Seventeen

MILES

After London and I finish our breakfast, she settles in on the sofa in the solarium, laptop set on her lap, Betsy at her feet, the fire roaring and the space heater going. She doesn't waste any time jumping right back into whatever it is she's working on, so I sneak off into my studio.

The generator is still chugging along since the power hasn't come back on yet, but all that means in here is that it's not as bright as it typically would be.

I check the pieces that have been cooling in the long-term oven, including the piece London and I made yesterday. It needs another day at least, but I'm hoping I can give it to her before we leave to drive her up to her parents' tomorrow. Not sure if that will work out or not.

The heaviest of the snow I think is behind us, and by this evening, it's supposed to be stopped altogether. It makes me antsy. It makes me unsettled and I can't stand this. She invited me to go with her, and I'm not sure what to do about that.

Do I pack a bag and stay? Celebrate Christmas with her family, a family who does not know me and very well likely might not approve?

Sure, I've come a long way from the kid growing up in the system.

I have a successful business. I make a very good living.

But London's family is so far out of my league. The fact that London has been here with me floors me. Wildest dreams and greatest fantasy come to life.

And part of me knows that the longer I hold on to her, the harder the fall when it's over.

That's how I went into this yesterday. Before I touched or kissed her. I didn't want to regret the time with her, not making a move, knowing full well that this is only a temporary situation.

But now yesterday feels like years ago and tomorrow feels imminent.

My plan was to fight for her. Until I realized fighting for her isn't exactly fair. What am I asking for? I can't move to New York, and how can I ask her to pick up and move here? Especially after such a short time. Add to that, the sobering thought that hit me square in the chest in the shower yesterday. The one that had me retreating.

What if she's like Piper, like everyone else, and one day decides she doesn't want me anymore and walks away?

Walking across the barn, I head into the gallery. There are a lot of pieces in here, but I know the one I want. It hit my mind the moment I woke up and saw her this morning. And though I would like to make her one of her own, create a piece just for her, I don't have the time if I want her to have it for tomorrow.

Lifting it up into my hands, I stare down at the colored glass, feeling the weight that's been sitting on my chest since she showed up growing heavier, more suffocating.

I'm terrified of loving her so much.

Blowing out a resigned breath, I wrap up the piece I want her to have, taping the bubble wrap and the brown paper around it.

The piece stays in my hand as I head back to my studio, determined to lose myself in some work for a while. I grab several different colored pillows, a specific design floating through my head. It'll take a lot of time to complete. Has a lot of detail, which will require a lot of concentration.

Exactly what I need.

I churn up the fire, placing my starting pillows in there and get to work. Music flows through the Bluetooth speakers I have set up for my phone, my mind lost in my piece, refusing to be pulled or drag in directions I can't allow it to go.

Sweat glides down my temple and I wipe it away with my forearm as I crouch down, pouring a strip of gold molten glass that will sparkle and shine when the piece is complete. Once it's laid the way I want it, I grab my blowtorch, heating up the end and taking my pliers, twisting the heated glass around a thin metal rod. Ever so carefully, I extract the rod, leaving an angled curl just as I want it.

Stepping back, I turn off the torch, staring at the piece and trying to figure out where I want to go next with it. The purple I'm envisioning will really set it off.

Especially against the gold.

I drop my hands to my hips, shifting and then stopping in my tracks as I catch sight of London leaning against the wall of the barn, arms folded over her chest, a fire in her eyes that instantly heats my blood.

"How long have you been standing there watching me?"

"A while," she admits. "I like watching you work. I don't think I've ever seen a sexier sight in my life."

London pushes off from the wall, sauntering toward me.

She's wearing tight yoga pants and a crop white long sleeve tee. Her hips move seductively, her shirt revealing her soft, toned abdomen. Her eyes are on mine, her lips slightly parted and my god, she's my siren's call. The one I will never stop wanting to answer, even if it has me falling headfirst into an ocean desperate to drown me.

Her hands run up my abs, her touch making my muscles clench and ripple. "You took off your shirt."

I nod, though I don't even remember doing it.

She leans in, licking a trail up from my navel to my nipple, tasting my sweat and salt on her tongue. She licks her lips, her eyes dark, the pulse at the base of her neck racing.

My hand grasps her neck, feeling that pulse against my palm as

I tilt her head back and to the side. "So beautiful, London. So fucking stunning I can hardly breathe when I look at you. You are the ultimate form of pain for me. The burning agony and the sweet torture of my life. I can't keep you but there is nothing I want more." I suck in a ragged breath, already reconciled, ready to tell her the words I've never told another living soul. "This feeling, this love I have for you... the way I want you, London is ripping me apart."

"Love isn't always pain, Miles."

That's where she's wrong. "In my world, it is."

Her eyes sparkle. "If love is pain, let me show you how good it can hurt."

I blow out the breath I didn't realize I was holding. Her blood is in my veins. A beautiful poison.

I lift her up, setting her down on one of the steel tables. My eyes dance about her face, a slow hypnotic beat courses through me. "You're the best present." My lips claim hers, my heart thumping in an uneven pattern as I removed her thin shirt. My fingers wrap around her narrow waist, sending goosebumps across her skin.

There's something about this moment, about the words I spoke and the almost forbidden way I want her but can't have her. The air crackles between us, my fingers tracing up the lines of her skin making her shudder. Fire zips down my spine, a bubbling desire building within that is impossible to control.

My lips mold to hers, teasing and taunting her tongue with mine as I kiss her. My hands come up, cupping her breasts, my thumbs skirting her hard nipples, straining through the satin of her bra. I roll them between my fingers, and she moans into my mouth.

All out of words, I kiss her deeper, pressing my body to hers.

My hands squeeze her ass, sliding her close to me as I stand between her spread thighs. Bending down, I bite her nipple through her bra, looking up into her eyes as she jerks and whimpers in pleasure. Pulling back, I rub over the wet spot I just created, loving how her breath comes out choppy and her cheeks flush.

Reaching behind her, I remove her bra, bringing my lips back down on her with another bite.

"Miles," she cries, her head falling back, her hands encircling my neck, twisting into the ends of my hair. My hand slides back down her waist, tugging off her leggings until she's naked before me. I've never fucked anyone in my studio. This was always my place for work. To escape anything. And in truth, other than my ex, I've never had a woman in my home.

But god, the things I want to do to London here.

With her legs spread, I slide two fingers inside her. She bucks against me, a long, languid moan fleeing her swollen lips.

My forehead drops to hers, my eyes open wide, watching as I finger her.

There is nothing more beautiful than the woman you love coming apart beneath your touch.

I pump her faster, but she's already so ready for me. A point she proves as she goes for my jeans, practically ripping them from my hips and shoving them down my legs. My cock springs free and in the next breath, I'm inside of her.

But instead of fucking her hard or deep or without mercy, I go slow. I stare into her eyes, I kiss her lips, I cup her face, and I love her body. And in doing so, a piece of me splinters off. Falls away. I don't even know what it is, but I feel something that's always been tight and restricting loosening.

"London," I whisper, my mouth attacking hers as I up my speed.

I can't fully explain what it is about her that's always drawn me to her. It was more than her popularity or sweet smile or stunning eyes. More than her sass or her brains. Lots of women have all of those, but none held me the way she does.

The way she always has.

My firefly. A bright spark of light in my otherwise dark sky.

My eyes close as everything I'm feeling becomes amplified. The feel of her around me. The sound of her heaving breathing and deep moans. The smell of her skin and taste of her sweat. All of it burned into my memory.

"I'm so close," she pants, her nails finding purchase in my back as I piston my hips into her, the table the most perfect fucking height in the history of sex.

My hand trails down her stomach, finding her clit and rubbing her. "Come for me, London. Fuck, baby, I want you to come so hard. I want you seeing stars. I want to feel your pussy convulse all over me as I fuck you, fuck you, fuck you."

A flurry of curses spin past her lips as she does just that. She explodes in my arms, shaking and shuddering, her knees quaking against my hips as I continue to ride into her, until my own orgasm takes hold. Waves of pleasure crash through me, so intense I'm momentarily blinded, yelling her name and squeezing her thighs to the point where I'm afraid I'll leave marks.

As our breathing slows and I take her in, I'm hit with the sucker punch. Followed by an untouchable truth. I will never love anyone the way I love this woman. And I have no idea what to do about that.

Chapter Eighteen

LONDON

Betsy howls like a bitch in heat as I put on Christmas music. I throw her a glare and she tosses one right back at me. "Girl, you gotta expand your musical pallet. There is more to life than Taylor Swift."

She's not buying it, barking again as Mariah Carey sings about how all she wants for Christmas is me. Well, you know what I mean. Miles has been quiet since our interlude in his studio earlier. We cleaned up and he put on a movie for me while he got working on dinner. A dinner he wouldn't let me help with.

Only, I'm not in the mood to watch a movie.

I'm too restless.

The snow stopped about an hour ago, and with it, the ticking of the countdown began.

He hasn't said as much, but I already know that when he drives me up to my parents' tomorrow morning, that's it. He's not staying. He's letting me go.

And wow. I mean, just wow. That seriously hurts.

I get it.

His life has certainly not been a bed of roses. Especially in the love department, but come the fuck on. I don't know what to say.

What to do. We live different lives in different states, and he's a man who is not all that adept at bridging gaps.

I'm not either, truth be told, but I wouldn't mind a little fight from him.

I think that's all it would take for me. A little fight.

"Miles," I shout as Michael Bublé croons an old classic with a new twist. "Come dance with me."

I get a grunt.

"Miles!"

His head peeks out from around the corner. "Yes, firefly?" Those sexy eyebrows bounce as do his full lips.

God, this man just fucking does it for me.

"Come dance with me, stud. I'm talking all the dips and twirls here."

"*All* the dips and twirls?"

"And whatever else you've got up those manly sleeves of yours."

Betsy barks, still annoyed at my choice in music.

Miles tosses her a treat as he swoops in, taking me in his arms and instantly tossing me back, my head dives down like a pelican going for a fish. My hands fly back, fingers scraping his pretty hard-wood floor, and suddenly, I'm upright again, my hair falling all over the place.

Miles throws me a devilish wink before taking me by the hand and twirling me in the direction of the fireplace. I belt out a laugh, my smile unstoppable as he spins me back, catching me with a hand on my lower back, digging me straight into his body.

"How was that?"

"Top it off with a kiss and it's my dream come true."

"Can't have anything but, now can we?" Then he does, in fact, top it off with a long, searing, pulse-racing, knee-weakening, kiss for the ages.

He drags himself away, our foreheads touching as we drop this down into a slow dance. He holds me close as we sway, the fire crackling and the music streaming, and it's perfect. Just so perfect. Except for the knock on the door.

Both of us jar back, eyes wide and blinking at each other.

Betsy goes nuts, barking and scratching at the door like this is the best thing to happen to her ever. A guest. Miles does not look pleased.

"I'm going to answer that," he announces.

"Okay."

"You wait here."

"I will."

He frowns, kissing my lips and then heading for the door. For some reason, something inside of me sinks faster than the Titanic. And that feeling of sinking or drowning or helplessness only increases as Miles opens the door and Fletcher is standing there, wearing a fucking livery uniform and an uncomfortable expression.

That is until his eyes home in on mine. "Miss London."

I might legit roll my eyes at that. Fletcher has known me since before I was even in diapers if you get my drift. Only I'm too shocked at his appearance to do much of anything other than gawk. "Fletcher?"

"Your father sent me," he explains, and somehow he ends up inside Miles's house, the door shuts and then an awkward silence hits all of us.

Miles's hurt gaze finds mine. "I thought you told your father I wanted to drive you up."

I swallow. "I did."

"Yes, sir," Fletcher starts. "But Mister Canterbury did not want to trouble you more than you've already been troubled. The snow stopped and the roads have been plowed enough for me to drive down here to collect Miss London." He steps forward, extending his hand to Miles, holding something in it that I hadn't seen before. "Here. With our many thanks for all that you've done for London."

Miles reaches out, numbly taking what looks to be an expensive bottle of something. Miles is a beer guy. Miles is not an expensive scotch guy. Miles frowns at the crystal in his hands, but somehow manages a nod and a thank you.

The gift is rude while being polite.

Miles didn't want a thank you. He doesn't care about expensive alcohol. He rescued me because that's who he is. And then everything else happened and now that thank you feels wrong.

Fucking Michael Bublé is still singing his freaking Christmasloving heart out as Miles stares into me and I stare back. *No*. It's all I can think. Just no. Not now. Not tonight. Not this soon.

Miles walks over to my phone that's hooked up to his Bluetooth speakers and disconnects it all, a sharp silence slicing through the room that nearly has me jumping in place. He hands me my phone, his motions brusque and edgy. "You should go gather your things."

Fuck.

"Miles—"

"I can do that for Miss London if need be."

I shake my head. Words fail me.

"I have to grab something from my workshop that I left in there earlier."

I shake my head some more. "Miles," I try again. "Stop."

"I want you to have it, London. Before you leave."

And my heart starts to bleed. Tiny pinpoint needle pricks stab into it. It's not a gush. It's not a deluge. It's a slow trickle, painful, agonizing, but slow. Mostly because I'm hoping this isn't happening. That Fletcher will go, and Miles and I will at least have tonight. Or maybe…

"Come with me, Miles."

His eyes meet mine and in them I watch as he shutters closed.

"Yes," freaking wonderful fucking Fletcher agrees. "Of course. Mister and Mrs. Canterbury would be delighted to have you join us for the holiday tomorrow. I'm sure they would relish the opportunity to thank you in person. It would be my honor to drive you back home after. My services won't be needed for Miss London as Miss Savannah will be heading back into New York and is planning to take Miss London with her."

A grunt. That's all Miles has got. "I'll be right back. Why don't you go upstairs and get your things? I'll meet you up there."

A sob lodges in my throat as I leave Fletcher standing here like a lost soldier while I head upstairs and Miles scurries off toward his workshop for who the hell knows what. I don't care. I want him up here with me so I can talk to him. So I can… so I can what? Tell him I'm not going back to New York?

Is that even rational? Is it even wanted?

Talk about presumptuous. Didn't he just say today that he can't keep me?

And what am I even thinking, giving up my apartment in New York and moving out here where I know no one? Where I've written the best opening six chapters of a book I've ever written?

Where the guy I want hasn't asked me to stay?

On shaky legs with my thoughts scattered, I make my way into the bedroom I initially slept in —the guestroom. My suitcases are still in here. I only moved a couple things into Miles's bedroom, but the majority of my things are here.

I pack them all up. It doesn't take me long. Just a few minutes. After all, I've only been here a couple of days. Not long at all. Not long enough to form the type of attachment to a man that I seem to already possess. Not nearly long enough to uproot one's life and relocate.

Especially for a man who is not exactly putting up a fight.

Tears cling to my eyes, burning the hell out of my nose, but I won't do it. I won't become that girl. Not right now, at least. That moment can come later in private.

Somehow, I find myself in his bedroom. I find myself tucking away all the things I brought in here. And like a juvenile, I spray his bed with my perfume.

Because I want the motherfucker to smell me tonight when he goes to sleep and I'm not here and he didn't say much more than he had to collect something from his workshop before I leave.

Before I leave!

Noise behind me has me staring straight ahead, drying out my eyes before I hold my breath and turn around. Miles is standing there, something in a long cardboard tube with a white cap in one hand and something smaller wrapped in brown paper in the other.

"These are for you."

Right. Well…

"Oh, firefly, don't cry."

Uh-huh. I nod. I swallow. I cry. Didn't I just freaking promise myself I wouldn't be this girl?

He crosses his room and takes me in his arms, tossing my perfume bottle on his bed like it's there to stay. "I'm sorry, London. But if I don't let you go now, I'm only going to get greedier. I can't lose you the way I've lost everything else that's ever mattered to me. You'll go back to New York and I'll still be here. That's how it works for me. That's how it's supposed to work for you. Your life is there. Mine is here."

How do you tell the guy you want to stay when he's not even offering that up as an option?

"Miles—"

"Be careful with these, okay? They're both fragile. But I don't want you to open them until tomorrow. Until Christmas. They're so, you know, you'll think back and remember your time here with me."

Is he joking with that? Think back? Like I need objects to remember him by?

Miles hugs me tighter, his voice growing raspy, hoarse, like just the art of pushing words past his vocal cords is the workout of a lifetime. "I knew it was going to be like this. I just" —hard swallow— "I just…" He can't even finish what he's trying to say, and I can't beg him to.

I can't beg him to change.

Instead he kisses my face, my closed eyes with my wet lashes. My nose that's running and likely red. My lips that hunger for him. That need him to say all the right things when everything he's saying is wrong.

He takes me by the hand, packages in tow and gathers my suitcases. I clutch my new presents while he carries my bags wordlessly down the stairs. Fletcher must sense the world of despair in the room because he mumbles something about putting my bags in the SUV and leaves in a rush.

"I'll have your car fixed and make sure you get it."

"I wanted you to come with me," I finally manage.

"I can't, London. Coming with you will kill me. If I can't keep you, then I have to let you go now."

"But—"

He steps forward, captures my mouth with his and tamps down any further argument I can mount. I can feel it. His desperation. His torment. A man who has never known the pleasure of love, only the pain. Only the loss. Only the fear.

Fletcher clears his throat and I reluctantly pull back. I don't know what to do right now other than go. Other than hope, it doesn't end this way. Other than muster up the strength to believe it won't. That there is, in fact, more for us. He just has to find a way to believe in it the way I do.

But as I look into his blue eyes one last time, I know that won't happen. He's letting me go. For good.

Chapter Nineteen

LONDON

I have no idea how long the ride up to my parents' house takes. It feels like an eternity and also brutally quick. I sit silently in the back of the SUV and Fletcher is smart enough not to try and fill it with empty banter. I feel like I've left my heart back there and I'm not sure how to get it back.

By the time we arrive, it's late and most of the lights are off, but as I walk into the kitchen behind Fletcher who is carrying my bags straight up to my bedroom, I find both of my parents and my sisters sitting around the kitchen in their pajamas drinking tea and munching on Christmas cookies.

"Santa's going to be pissed when he finds you're eating all his cookies."

All heads swivel in my direction and I don't have to force a smile even when my insides feel like they're being ripped apart. I'm happy to be here. I missed my family. This is where I belong. Sorta.

One by one, they all stand up. Loud, affectionate 'welcome homes' and 'we're so happy you're okay' and 'now Christmas is complete' surround me as do their hugs and kisses. I sink into that. Meld into their love and push everything else back.

I go for the plate of cookies and accept a cup of tea.

Chamomile, my favorite. With any luck, it'll knock me out.

Especially as my sister Charlie adds a few hearty plops of brandy to it with a knowing wink. I must look about as good as I feel.

I take a few sips, still clutching the presents Miles gave me in my hands because I wouldn't let Fletcher take them upstairs. I nibble on a cookie and listen while my mom spews stuff about a baby shower for Savannah while I promise to help with it.

But all too soon, I tell them I'm tired and after I kiss them each good night, ignoring their questioning and concerned looks, I take my tea and my presents, and I find my room.

Setting the objects down on the bed, I stare at them for the longest of moments. That is until I hear a small knock on my door followed by it opening without waiting on my reply. "London?"

"I'm fine, Charlie."

"That's a lie," Savannah states, walking into my room uninvited because that's just her way. "Tell us what's up. I talked to Rina this morning and she said you looked really happy with the guy. With Miles, right?"

"Miles? You didn't tell me his name was Miles," Charlie says, sitting on my bed as does Savannah who tries to make herself as comfortable as she can with a small bowling ball protruding from her belly. "This is the same Miles?"

I snicker, staring at my sisters. Charlie looks so much like me we could be twins other than the five-year age gap between us. Savannah too, well, other than the bowling ball. "How do you remember that?"

She hitches up a shoulder. "Because we talked about it that night. We stayed up eating peanut butter and fluff from the containers and you told me about the guy who kissed you and walked off right after. His name isn't the most common." Another shrug. "I remembered."

"Well, yeah. It's him."

"Are these from him or presents for us?" Savannah asks, shifting on my bed on the opposite side from Charlie while I continue to stand at the foot, staring down at the presents.

"From him," I whisper, already getting stupidly emotional. "He said not to open them until tomorrow."

"Did you invite him to come for Christmas? Or was this a quick and dirty affair?"

I look up, glaring at Savannah and she throws her hands up instantly.

"Crap. You really like him a lot."

"I didn't intend to fall for the guy within a span of forty-eight hours. I didn't even know something like that was possible."

"London, you fell for him back in high school," Charlie asserts with that knowing gleam in her eyes. "This was just rekindling something that had already been there."

Maybe. But that still doesn't make me feel better.

"I did invite him to come." I blow out a heavy breath, sagging onto the end of the bed and picking at the brown paper of the smaller present.

Things were going so well. I mean, *so* well. We were laughing and having amazing sex, and just being with him felt so good. Like best ever good. Like pieces I didn't even realize were missing fell into place.

That's what he felt like.

The last piece to my completed puzzle. I know what I am without him. What my picture looks like. But once you put that final piece in, the entire puzzle comes together in a perfect way.

"Why didn't he come?" Charlie again.

His story isn't mine to tell. I shake my head. His story isn't mine to tell.

"Not an easy thing to make work," I go with instead.

"Do you think he felt the same way you feel about him back?" Savannah prods.

I look up, meeting my sisters' concerned gazes and this time, I nod. Because I do think he did. I saw it in the way he looked at me. In the way he touched me. In the words he said to me. I felt it in all of it. But at the end of the day, Fletcher showed up suddenly and unexpectedly and Miles just shut down.

Maybe if he had driven me up, he'd be here now with me, but I'll never know because he didn't fight. And hell, that hurts.

"Well, it's officially tomorrow," Savannah announces. "It's after midnight and since we're not waiting on Santa, or the guy it seems, open them up."

"Sav," Charlie admonishes. "She should do that alone."

Savannah turns back to me. "Do you want to do that alone? Or do you want sisterly support?"

I honestly don't know. I don't know what he gave me. "Stay," I decide, because maybe I won't fall apart if my sisters are here with me. At least, that's what I'm hoping.

I start with the smaller object first, removing the brown paper with care and then slowly unfurling the thick barrier of the bubble wrap. Finally, once it's revealed, I hold it in my hand, my throat thick and my eyes watery with unshed tears.

"An ornament?" Charlie asks, perplexed.

"He blows glass for a living. He makes beautiful pieces. He made this."

"It's a heart," Savanah chimes in. "A violet heart. It's beautiful. It almost looks like a prism the way the lines of it go. I bet it sparkles on the tree against the lights."

I bet she's right.

"Open the next one," Charlie demands, and I reluctantly set down my pretty heart-shaped ornament. Popping open the white plastic cap on the tube, I turn it upside down and a piece of rolled-up sketch paper slides onto the bed, unrolling a little as it goes.

Both Charlie and Savannah gasp when they catch sight of the image, their hands covering their mouths. It's one he must have drawn when we were sitting on the sofa together. When I was writing, and he was drawing. It's a charcoal sketch of me, wrapped up in a blanket, curled up on his sofa, watching the fire with a small smile etched on my lips.

A purple piece of paper floats onto the bed as I stare at the exquisite rendering.

"What's that? Did he write you something?"

I swallow past the lump in my throat and pick it up, my eyes blurry as I read aloud, "Merry Christmas, Firefly. I'll never be happy you got hurt, but you crashing your car was the best thing to ever happen to me because you're the best thing to ever happen to me. All my love, Miles."

"Shit. Damn."

"Yeah," Charlie agrees with Savannah. "All of that."

They both reach out, touching me, offering me their comfort as I fall apart, unable to stop it. A sob cleaves a path from my chest just as the first of my tears start to fall.

"Stupid boys. Stupid perfect presents."

"Yes. That too," they both say. "Are you going to call him?" Charlie asks.

"I can't. I don't even have his freaking cell phone number to text him a thanks because I never got it. This was his goodbye. It's done. It's over."

"No, it's not," Savannah says adamantly. "This dude is the real deal, London. You don't just let that go. You don't just walk away."

"I didn't walk away—" I start to protest, but she quickly waves me off.

"Semantics. You need to go back to him. You need to tell him you're not accepting goodbye and he needs to get over whatever his hang-ups are."

I think on that for a moment. Like really think about it.

Miles does have hang-ups. He never thought he was good enough. Never felt he was worthy of me or anything special in his life.

Love has only ever hurt him.

So can I blame him for not coming with me?

Hell, I'm scared too, but I have to imagine it's a million times worse for him. What did he say? *Coming with you will kill me. If I can't keep you, then I have to let you go now.*

Oh Miles.

"You know what, you're right. You're absolutely freaking right," I tell them.

"I always am." Charlie and I both roll our eyes.

Charlie and I both roll our eyes.

"Whatever. I'm going to go after him. I'll spend Christmas morning here with the family and then I'm going to drive back down to him. Tell him that I want to be with him."

"Damn straight. Fight for what you want," Charlie says on a big smile.

I will. But suddenly, I'm terrified.

Maybe he's right. Maybe it is easier this way.

What happens if I show up at his house and he turns me away?

I fall flat on my side, closing my eyes. For the first time, I understand what Miles meant by love is pain. I just wish he knew it didn't have to be this way. I guess that's just something I'll have to show him.

Chapter Twenty

LONDON

Bright sunlight is not my friend right now. I fell asleep who the hell knows what time and now I'm up, earlier than I'd like to be. My sisters sat with me for a little while longer before they both went to bed. Now here it is, Christmas morning and my face probably looks like I'm having some sort of allergic reaction and my insides don't exactly feel much better.

I vowed to myself last night that regardless of what Miles does, I wasn't going to let my hurt and nerves over a guy ruin my Christmas with my family. I'll drive down later today. He said he has no plans for Christmas and while part of me is beyond excited and exhilarated over the idea of what I plan to do, the other part of me is scared out of my mind.

His incredible picture is still sitting on the bed, re-rolled into the packaging it came in. The stunning ornament too because I didn't have it in me to look at them anymore. I have no idea what to do with them now.

Do I want that ornament on our family tree?

Um. Kinda yes, because it's too pretty and special to be left out, but also no because every time I look at it, it'll just be a reminder of the man I'm trying really hard not to think about until later.

Dragging my ass out of bed, I head into my bathroom, running a washcloth under cold water and pressing it to my face until some of the redness and puffiness dissipates. I rub in some face cream so at least I have a bit of healthy-looking glow, brush out the tangles from my hair, brush my teeth and then get into my Christmas pajamas because it's fucking Christmas and I'm going to celebrate that.

But I also re-pack my bags.

I stuff everything inside, including his presents to me. I lay out an outfit I want to wear when I go to him and that makes me smile and squeal just a little because I happen to know for a fact, I look sensational in this sweater that has pretty sparkly beads on it in green, red, and white against the thin black cashmere.

Miles will drool over it.

Because Miles wants me. He's just too afraid to take the step.

The house is still quiet as I walk through the dining room and the great room. Sounds in the kitchen draw my attention as does the smell of baking muffins. The moment I step into the kitchen, I find my father sitting at the counter, hovering over his cup of barely steaming coffee, his eyes dark and tired.

"Daddy?"

He raises his head, and I catch the glimmer lurking beneath the fatigue.

"Come and sit down, London. Tell me all about this Miles guy."

I blow out a breath, followed by a roll of my eyes. "Merry Christmas to you too. What do you need to know about Miles?"

"If he's a good man or not. If he's worthy of my little girl. He rescued my daughter from a blizzard and brought her into his home. You went to high school with him, but I have no recollection of him, and I thought I knew all your friends. But most of all, you showed up last night and it looked like someone had stolen all the light from your eyes, but this morning it seems to be back despite the nice cut you have on your forehead."

I bluster out a sigh, sinking down against the large island counter. I can smell the muffins and before Greta, our chef, has a heart attack, I go over to the oven, slip on her mitts and remove the muffins, setting them on the cooling rack.

"She's going to cut you in your sleep. Christmas be damned."

My father looks unconcerned. "I never liked blueberry."

I shake my head. "Daddy!"

"Talking to my daughter one on one is worth burned muffins."

"You say that until your pregnant daughter comes down."

My father blanches and then meets my eyes with an indifferent shrug. "I've got at least twenty minutes before that happens. Talk to me, London. Tell me about this man."

"Daddy…" I sag onto a stool, ripping off the oven mittens and throwing them onto the counter one at a time. "He found me. I told you all this already. I passed out and he brought me back to his house."

"And…" He trails off with the cock of an eyebrow that says he knows I'm withholding.

"And he's amazing. Kind and sweet and considerate. He's an artist. Makes beautiful pieces out of glass. I knew him back in high school and I just… Daddy, after Christmas breakfast and we open all our presents, I'm going to borrow a car and drive back down to him."

My father takes a sip of his coffee, his eyes on mine. "Because you want to be with him?"

I nod. I smile with teeth and everything.

"He was good to you then? Took care of you?"

I roll my eyes. "Yes. He was good to me. He cooked for me and brought ice for my knee and bandaged my head. He's a good man. I swear. You'll really like him."

"Do you love him?"

I laugh. It's awkward. It's weird sounding. "Why the hell do you ask that? It was only a couple of days."

"Because I'm wondering if I should call the police on the man who has been parked in my driveway since before dawn broke."

"What?" I jump up to my feet, spinning around though I can't see into the driveway from the kitchen. I turn back to my father. "Are you serious?"

"I am. Our alarm company sent an alert before five this morning. He's been out there, sitting in his car and silently waiting. A man doesn't go to such extremes unless he's screwed up in the head or is in love enough to want to repair that screw-up."

"Dad…"

"Tell me, London."

I look my father in the eyes. The same hue as mine. "I think I love him."

"Then maybe bring him a muffin. He's got to be hungry. After that, bring him inside so I can meet the man my baby girl has fallen for."

I suck in a breath, walking over and wrapping my arms around my father's neck. "Thanks, Daddy."

"That's what I'm here for, honey. Always. But this man. He came here really early for you. I'm guessing things didn't go well when you left yesterday?"

I sigh again. Excited and hurt and excited all over again. "Not really. I asked him to come with me and he got cold feet. But I think he wanted to. He just hasn't had it easy before."

"He loves you? The way you deserve?"

"Yeah. He does." I know he does.

"Breakfast will be ready soon. Greta is going to murder me in my sleep apparently if I don't let her back into the kitchen. I have to warn your mother that there's a man outside so get a move on."

"I'm on my way out now."

"And London?" I turn back over my shoulder. "Bring him inside. It's freezing out there. His dog too. If he's going to be yours, I can't have them sitting in the driveway."

Dammit, Daddy!

"I love you."

"You too, baby girl."

I cross the kitchen and kiss his cheeks before leaving out the way I came in last night. I throw on a coat and my boots, stepping out into the frigid air. The morning light is muted, still hazy with the remnants of the storm. I came here last night with a broken heart in tow and now staring at the cold truck in the driveway, the barely-there rumbling of the engine, I don't care what Miles has to say.

He's here.

He drove up here, likely in the middle of the night. For me.

As I approach, I find both Miles and Betsy fast asleep inside, one of Taylor Swift's earlier albums strumming from the speakers, filtering out into the dawn. "If you could see that I'm the one who understands you. Been here all along, so why can't you see. You belong with me."

Thanks, Taylor. I, for real, couldn't agree more.

I knock on the window and smile as Miles stirs with a jolt. He jumps upright in his seat, glancing at Betsy who has barely moved, her eyes still closed though her tail starts to wag a little. Then he flips around quickly in my direction, finding me smiling outside his window.

His eyes blink and then does so again. He scrubs his hands over his face, wiping the sleep away, and then he starts to roll down his window but thinks better of it and slides it back up, choosing to unlock his car and open the door instead.

I step back, giving him space, and once he's standing before me, his eyes on mine and his smirk in place, I fall so hard for this man.

So totally in love.

"I didn't know how to do this," he starts without any preamble.

So completely.

"I was standing in my house for like ten minutes after you left, and both Betsy and I knew it was a mistake to let you go. The house was too quiet. My chest too empty. I couldn't stand it, London. It was like the world was crushing me and the only thing to give me breath was you. I fucked up by letting you go. I fucked up so bad and I knew it. I was scared and stubborn and did I mention fucking scared? Nothing in my life has ever lasted. No one has ever loved me long enough to stick around and I panicked."

"Then what?"

He chuckles, running a hand through his hair the way he likes to do when he's a bit off-balance. A bit flustered and unsure. "Then I got in my truck and before I knew it, it was too late to show up at your parents' home. We went to a motel and slept for a couple of hours, but I wanted to be here when you woke up."

"Why?" I ask, stepping into him, not really needing the answer but craving it all the same. My hand touches his face, my heart is already wound with his.

His hands cradle my face, his glowing eyes searching mine, bouncing back and forth, his expression so serious.

"Because I love you, London. I've loved you my whole life. Since I was a kid and I first laid eyes on you. I was crazy to let you go. To let my fear get the best of me. You own my heart, London Canterbury. It's yours and everything else is secondary. My house and work are in Vermont. Yours is in New York. We're in two different worlds, but I can't lose you. I've lost enough in my life and you're my final straw. My non-option. Tell me what I have to do to keep you and I will do it. Anything."

"Anything?"

He grins as I cock an eyebrow. "Dammit, yeah. I'd do anything to keep you. To make you mine."

"Well, thank goodness for that. Because I was actually going to drive down after breakfast with my family and tell you I wasn't letting you go. I'm wondering how you'd feel if I came back with you after Christmas? You know, spent New Year's with you? See how things went. What do you think?"

He blinks at me, a little stunned, I think. He was gearing up for a fight I have no interest in. I'm his.

"Are you serious?" He chuckles, his smile growing, his dimples out in full force. "Yes. Hell yes! Come. Stay with me. Never leave."

"Careful, Miles. I might take you up on that."

I want to be there writing in his solarium and I want to watch him work in his shop. I want to make love to him in every freaking square inch of his home, and let me tell you, that's a lot of square inches to cover.

It's simple really…

"I love you."

His entire face lights up. "You do?"

I giggle a little at his awestruck expression. Then I nod.

"I love you," he whispers. "I never saw you coming, but I'm so fucking grateful you did."

"I don't need New York. I just need you. I can work from anywhere as my parents like to remind me."

His lips rain down on mine, his hands holding me close as he steals my breath and devours my happy smiles.

"Thank you for the presents," I murmur into him. "I love them. They're beautiful."

"You're beautiful." He kisses me again. "Were you really coming back to me?"

I nod against him as the most breathtaking smile sweeps back over him.

Suddenly it hits me. No one has ever come back for him. They've only left. I'm his first and I'll never walk away from him. Never.

"I'm glad I got to you first. I should have never let you go after that first kiss and I sure as hell shouldn't have let you leave last night. Just one kiss from you could never be enough."

Reaching up on my toes, I kiss him again, wrapping my arms around his neck and holding on for dear life. His is the love of a lifetime. The one every little girl dreams of having.

Him. This man. I never stood a freaking chance.

Epilogue

London
One year later

"MILES!" I shout, running around the upstairs and digging through every freaking drawer in this place. "I can't find it. Where the Christmas is my black beaded sweater?"

"It's in your drawer," he replies from somewhere downstairs. I roll my eyes. Did he really just say in my drawer when I have like ten?

"Super unhelpful," I call back only to hear him chuckle.

"Just wear what you're wearing. It's getting late."

I growl under my breath. I have to wear that sweater. Doesn't he get it? It's the sweater I wore on our first Christmas together last year. The one I had specifically set out that makes not only my tits look fantastic, but my skin glow and my eyes pop.

Dammit, Miles. I need to wear that sweater.

It's been the best year ever and I want to celebrate that.

After Miles came in for Christmas breakfast with my family last year, he ended up staying for two more days. My parents were crazy for him instantly. My sisters and their husbands too. Betsy was the hit of the holiday though and had everyone eating out of her paw.

Greta even baked special treats just for her.

After that, we drove back down to his house together and that was sort of it. I mean, I did go back to New York, but that was only for a week and that was only to clean out my apartment and say goodbye to a few people.

Rina had already moved to Boston and since she is my main person besides my sisters, it wasn't as hard to leave the city I'd been living in for eight years as one might think. Then again, I was coming back here. To my mountain man. To my Vermont oasis. To what I now affectionately refer to as my office, which is the solarium. Miles even surprised me by buying a beautiful desk for me and rearranged the furniture so it would be my space.

He never actually asked me to move in.

It was just how we talked about things. The way the words flowed from us. It was kind of like once we said I love you, that was it. The moving in and being together part just became a forgone conclusion. Something we did and never thought twice about or looked back on.

For the last two months, Miles has been a very busy worker bee. His ornaments evidently are in high demand, and he was pretty much living in his shop.

That actually worked out well for me because my Christmas book, Just One Kiss, came out at the end of November. It's our story as I like to think. The one I started writing when Miles rescued me.

"London!" Miles shouts as I'm digging through one of his drawers. "Come on, Firefly. I want to give you your present before we leave."

"I need my sweater!"

"Wear the cream dress. It looks beautiful on you."

I glance down at the dress I threw on while searching for my sweater. "I look like a church mouse in it."

"Then wear something sexy beneath and get your adorable ass down here."

"I am wearing something sexy beneath," I grumble, though I'm smirking. That's part of his present, though he doesn't get to unwrap it until tonight. "Fine!" I bellow, slamming the stupid drawer shut and stomping down the stairs in my heels.

Miles and Betsy are waiting at the foot for me. She's wearing an adorable red sweater I had made for her and Miles is wearing a dark blue sweater—because the man would rather die than wear Christmas colors—and dark gray slacks. His thick hair is brushed back and his glasses are on.

He looks so damn yummy I can hardly stand it.

He greets me with a kiss that I quickly return, though I'm still pouting. "I wanted my sweater. That's our sweater, Miles."

He grins like I'm adorable, kissing the tip of my nose. "I know, baby. But you look gorgeous in this."

"It's not the same."

"Let's open our presents and see if that cheers you up."

"What about Betsy's present?"

He shakes his head, tossing her a treat on her bed by the kitchen that she quickly retreats to. Thankfully, as much as I love Taylor, Betsy has broadened her musical pallet and readily accepts my Christmas music.

Miles takes my hand and leads me over to the solarium, sitting me on the sofa we first made love on. Outside the window is a sea of white and forest green. So beautiful and picturesque, although mother nature decided that this year we deserved some sun instead of blizzard conditions.

"Can I give you mine first?" I ask, and Miles frowns but quickly acquiesces with a bob of his head.

I hand him two things, both wrapped in bright red paper. He lets out a bemused chuckle as he takes in the Santa and reindeer and then has at it, ripping away at the paper. The first gift is a signed hardcover of our book, Just One Kiss. It's in a special cover I had made, a picture of us that was taken last Christmas at my parents'.

He runs his hand along the smooth cover, a small smile curling up his lips. "Open it," I instruct, and his eyes quickly come up to mine before diving back down to the book.

He flips open the cover, reading what I wrote for him. "Sometimes all it takes to fall in love is Just One Kiss. With all my heart, I love you. – London." He closes it, his eyes glassy and mine are already starting to water. "Jesus, London. This is incredible. My present isn't half as thoughtful."

I choke out a watery laugh. "I don't care. This is us, Miles. You're all I need." He leans in and gives me a sweet kiss. "Open the next."

This one is bigger, softer, and the moment he opens it, I see his eyes rolling. "Red?"

I nod.

"It'll clash with your eyes."

"You only have to wear it today."

He frowns, staring down at the red Christmas sweater I got him more as a joke than anything else. "I'll put it on when we get to your parents' house. Not a second before."

I grin like a stupid girl in love because only a guy who really loves you would dare to wear a bright red sweater that has fucking Santa and green glittery ornaments on it. Still, it's a terrible holiday tradition in my family. Ugly Christmas sweaters for the men, and last year, Miles didn't have one.

"I love the first present."

I laugh, wrapping my arms around his neck and kissing him. "I'm glad. There's more, but they're already at my parents' place. I had them shipped there."

He cocks an eyebrow. "Just so we can bring them back home after?"

"You have to have something to open under the tree, Miles. Don't be such a spoilsport."

"Yes ma'am." He gives me another kiss and then places a large white box on my lap, tied together with a lavender bow.

So simple. So pretty. So Miles.

I tug on the ribbon, releasing the bow and setting it aside. Then

I remove the lid and stare down inside the box for a solid minute, trying to understand just what the hell I'm looking at.

"Careful," he warns. "It's delicate."

"Ummmm." I glance up at him, my eyebrows pinched, and then back down to the box. "This is my present?"

"Yes."

"Miles."

I reach in, touching the black cashmere.

"Like I said, it's delicate."

"It's my sweater. The one I was just searching all over the goddamn house for."

"I know. Do you like it?"

My eyebrows hit my hairline, and an incredulous pinch of my lips takes over. I'm honestly not sure what to do in this situation. The man re-gifted my sweater back to me.

My hands wrap around the soft material, lifting it out and it's only then that I realize there's more to it than that. The sweater is wrapped around something that does, in fact, feel delicate. Fragile even.

Shifting on the sofa, I set the sweater down carefully, folding back the layers of fabric to find a beautiful blue heart-shaped ornament inside. A smile hits my lips.

"I gave you the purple one last year and I thought maybe it would be our new tradition."

Wow, he's cute. And nervous if his expression is anything to go by. He was worried I wouldn't like it, but I love it.

"Miles," I whisper, my voice thick. "It's gorgeous."

I pick it up, twirling the heart in my hand only to discover that when I turn it over, it's got a large hole in the front. And sitting inside is a pretty red box. I stare at it, stunned, unable to move or breathe.

Miles helps me by taking the ornament from my hands and removing the box. Then he's down on one knee in front of me, his hands in my lap and his face directly before mine.

"London Amelia Canterbury, I don't know how to thank you. All my life I never felt like I deserved much. And anything I had, well, it never lasted long. But then you blew back into my life and everything changed. You've given me so much this past year. Your heart. Your smiles. Your warmth. Your life. Your love. All of them I cherish. All of them I cannot live without. Will you marry me, London?"

He opens the box to reveal a large, stunning oval diamond set on a band of diamonds.

He takes the ring from the box and slips it onto my finger, his eyes bright and earnest and so full of love. Without thinking, I throw my arms around his neck and kiss the hell out of him. He laughs, kissing me back with equal ardor.

"Is that a yes?" he asks against my lips.

"Yes." I laugh in return. "Didn't I say that already?"

"Um. No. I would have remembered you saying yes after I asked you to marry me."

I giggle like crazy. "Yes, Miles. I'll marry you. I'll marry you tomorrow and every day after that. I'll marry you forever."

**THE END

Thank you for reading Miles and London's story. If you enjoyed it, please consider leaving a review. Keep reading for a glimpse at Reckless Love and The Edge of Temptation.

Sign up for my newsletter and receive a free book!

Also by J. Saman

Wild Love Series:

Reckless Love

Love to Hate Her (Wild Minds Duet 1)

Hate to Love Him (Wild Minds Duet 2)

Crazy to Love You

Love to Tempt You

The Edge Series:

The Edge of Temptation

The Edge of Forever

The Edge of Reason

Start Again Series:

Start Again

Start Over

Start With Me

Las Vegas Sin Series:

Touching Sin

Catching Sin

Darkest Sin

Standalones:

Just One Kiss

Love Rewritten

Beautiful Potential

Forward - FREE

End Of Book Note

If you haven't read me before, this is the part of the book where I free associate about the story (unedited). I was not planning on writing a Christmas story this year. I literally dreamt this story and when I woke up, I started writing. And two weeks later, it was finished. Super quick for me.

I can't tell you how much I love Miles and London. Both individually and together. I liked that Miles was a bit broken but so in love with London. I loved how they had a history and obviously both liked each other in high school though neither admitted it. I liked how London was quirky and funny and just so herself, consequences be damned. She's someone I would really want to be friends with.

I didn't want this story to have twists or villains. I didn't want it to be complicated. I really just wanted to tell a story about two people who were always meant to be. It's not always easy to get out of our own way sometimes and in this case, fate needed to step in and lend a hand.

I hope this story made you laugh and swoon and just feel good. That's all I wanted from this. I think we could all use some of that right now.

If you have read my The Edge series you will recognize Rina's name. She is set to get her own story coming in 2021 and I gave you chapter 1 of The Edge of Temptation (book 1 in that series of standalones) after this note.

Thank you again for reading Just One Kiss. I appreciate you so very much!!

XO ~ J. Saman

Reckless Love

Prologue
  Lyric

I can't stop staring at it. Reading the two short words over and over again ad nauseum. They're simple. Essentially unimpressive if you think about it. But those two words mean everything. Those two words dive deep into the darkest depths of my soul, the part I've methodically shut off over the years, and awaken the dormant volcano. How can two simple words make this well of emotions erupt so quickly?

Come home.

I don't recognize the number the text came from. It shows up as Unknown. But I don't have to recognize it. I know who it's from. Instinctively, I know. At least, my body does, because my heart rate is through the roof. My stomach is clenched tight with violent, poorly concealed, sickly butterflies. My forehead is clammy with a sheen of sweat and my hands tremble as they clutch my phone.

It's early here in California. Not even dawn, but I'm awake. I'm always awake, even when I'm not, and since my phone has, unfortunately, become another appendage, it's consistently with me.

It's a New York area code.

Goddammit! I suck in a deep, shuddering breath of air that does absolutely nothing to calm me, then I respond in the only way I can.

Me**: *Who is this?***

The message bubble appears instantly, like he was waiting for me. Like there is no way this is a wrong number. Like his fingers couldn't respond fast enough.

Unknown: ***You know who this is. Come home.***

I don't respond. I can't. I'm frozen. It's been four years. Four fucking years. And this is how he reaches out? This is how he contacts me? I slink back down into my bed, pulling the heavy comforter over my head in a pathetic attempt to protect myself from the onslaught of emotions that consume me. I tuck my phone against my chest, over what's left of my fractured heart.

I'm hurting. I'm angry. I'm so screwed up and broken, and yet, I'm still breaking. How is that even possible? How can a person continue to break when they're already broken? How can a person I haven't seen in four years still affect me like this?

I want to throw the traitorous device into the wall and smash it. Toss it out my window as hard as I can and hope it reaches the Pacific at the other end of the beach, where it will be swept away, never to return. But I don't. Because curiosity is a nefarious bitch. Because I have to know why the man who was my everything and now my nothing is contacting me after all this time, asking me to come home.

Unknown***: I'm sitting here in my old room, on my bed, and I can't focus. I can't think about what I need to be thinking about. So, I need you to come home.***

I shake my head as tears line my eyes, stubbornly refusing to fall but obscuring my vision all the same. Nothing he's saying makes sense to me. Nothing. It's completely nonsensical, and yet, it's not. I still know him well enough to understand both what he's saying and what he's not.

Me: ***Why?***

Unknown***: Because I need you to.***

Me: ***I can't. Too busy with work.***

That's sort of a lie. I mean, I *am* headed to New York for the Rainbow Ball in a few days. But he doesn't need to know that. And I do not want to see him. I absolutely, positively, do not.

Unknown: ***My dad had a stroke***

My eyes cinch shut, and I cover them with one hand. I can't breathe. A gasped sob escapes the back of my throat, burning me with its raw taste. God. Now what the hell am I going to do? I love his father. Jesus Christ. How can I say no to him now? How can I avoid this the way I so desperately need to? *Shit.*

Me: ***I'm sorry. I didn't know. Is he okay?***

Unknown: ***He'll live, but he's not great. He's in the ICU. Worse than he was after the heart attack.***

I shake my head back and forth. I can't go. I can't go home. I was there two months ago to visit my parents and my sister's family. I have work—so much freaking work that I can barely keep up. I don't want to see him. I won't survive it. I'll see him, and I'll feel everything I haven't allowed myself to feel. I'll be sucked back in.

Things are different now.

They are. My situation has changed completely, but I never had the guts to call him and tell him that. Mostly because I was hurt. Mostly because I felt abandoned and brushed off. Mostly because I was terrified that it wouldn't matter after all this time apart. If I see him now, knowing how much has changed…Shit. I just…Fuck. I can't.

I don't know what to do.

I'm drenched in sweat. The blanket I sought refuge in is now smothering me. I'm relieved his father is alive. I still speak to him once a month. Wait, let me amend that—he still *calls* me once a month. And we talk. Not about Jameson. Never about him. Only about me and my life. I'm a wreck that Jameson is contacting me. I can't play this game. I never could. It was all or nothing with him.

Unknown: ***I miss you.***

I stare at the words, read them over again, then respond too quickly, ***Liar.***

Unknown: ***Never. I miss you so goddamn much.***

I think I just died. Everything inside me has stopped. My heart is not beating. My breath has stalled inside my chest, unable to be expelled. My mind is completely blank. And when everything comes back to life, I'm consumed with an angry, caustic fury I never knew I was capable of.

Unknown: ***Are you still there?***

Me: ***What do you want me to say?***

Unknown: ***I don't know. I'm torn on that. Please come home.***

Me: ***Why?***

Unknown: ***Because I need you. Because he needs you. Because I was always too busy obsessing over you to fall for someone else. Because I need to know if I'm making a mistake by hoping.***

I shake my head vigorously, letting out the loudest, shrillest shriek I can muster. It's not fucking helping, and I need something to help. Clamoring out of bed, I hurry over to the balcony doors, unlocking them and tossing them open wide.

Fresh air. I need fresh air. Even Southern California fresh air. A burst of salty, ocean mist hits me square in the face, clinging to the sweat I'm covered in. It's still dark out. Dawn is not yet playing with the midnight-blue sky.

I stare out into the black expanse of the ocean, listen to the crashing of the waves and sigh. I knew about him. I would be lying if I said I hadn't Facebook-stalked him a time or twenty over the years. Forced myself to hate him with the sort of passion reserved for political figures and pop stars. But this? Saying he misses me?

Me: ***Seeing me won't change that. But if you're asking, you are.***

He responds immediately, and I can't help but grin a little at that. *You still care about me, Jameson Woods.* When I catch the traitorous thought, I shut it down instantly. Because if he cared, if his texted words meant anything, then I wouldn't be here, and he wouldn't be there, and this bullshit four a.m. text conversation wouldn't be happening.

Unknown: ***I'm not asking. Seeing you might change***

everything. But more than that, I need you here with me. My father would want to see you. Come home.

I hate him. I hate him. I hate him!

Me: *I can't come home. Stop using your father to manipulate me.*

Unknown: *It's the only play I have. You can come home. I know you can. Are you seeing someone? Before you respond, any answer other than no might kill me right now.*

I growl, not caring if anyone walking by hears. How can he do this to me? How can he be so goddamn selfish? Doesn't he know what he put me through? That I still haven't found my way back after four years? I shouldn't reply. I should just throw my phone away and never look back.

Me: *No. And you're a bastard.*

Unknown: *YES. I Am! Please. I am officially begging. Really, Lee. I'm not even bullshitting. I'm a mess. Please. Please. Please!!!!*

Me: *...*

Unknown: *What does that mean?*

Me: *It means I'm thinking. Stop!*

My eyes lock on nothing, my mind swirling a mile a minute.

Lee. He called me Lee. That nickname might actually hurt the most. And now he's asking me to come home. Jameson Woods, the man I thought was my forever, is asking me to come home to see him. And for what? To scratch a long-forgotten itch? To assuage some long-abandoned guilt over what he did? Why would I fall for that?

I sigh again because I know why. It's the same reason I never bring men home. It's the same reason I haven't given up this house even though I don't fully live in it anymore and it's far from convenient. It's the same reason I continued this conversation instead of smashing my phone.

Jameson Woods.

The indelible ink on my body. The scar on my soul. The fissure in my heart.

Unknown: ...

I can't help the small laugh that squeaks out as I lean forward and prop my elbows on the edge of the railing. The cool wind whips through my hair, and I hate that I feel this way. That I'm entertaining him the way I am.

Me: **What does that mean?**

Unknown: **It means I'm getting impatient. Please. I need you to come home. I know I'm a bastard. I know I shouldn't be asking you this. But I am.**

Unknown: **Aren't you at least a little curious?**

YES!

Me: **NO!!!!!!! And bastard doesn't cover you.**

Unknown: **Please. It's spinning out of control, and I need to see you. I need to know.**

Me: **You already know.**

Unknown: **About you?**

Me: **Yes, or you wouldn't be texting me at four in the morning.**

Unknown: **It's seven here. Does that mean you'll come?**

Me: ...

Unknown: ...

Me: **Yes.**

My phone slips from my fingers, clanging to the hard surface of my balcony floor. My phone buzzes again, a little louder now since the sound is reverberating off the ground. I don't pick it up. I don't look down. I don't care if he's thanking me or anything else he comes up with. I don't care. I don't want to know.

Because I'm busy getting my head on straight.

Locking myself down.

I'm worried about his father and I want to see him, want to make sure he's okay with my own two eyes.

I'll go home and I'll see him. I'll see him, and I'll do the one thing I was never able to do before. I'll say goodbye. My eyes close and I allow myself to slip back. To remember every single moment we had together. To indulge in the sweet torture that, if I let it, will rip me apart piece by piece. Because I know what I'm in for, and I know that once I step foot off that airplane, nothing will ever be right again.

Want to know what happened with Jameson and Lyric and if the'll ever get their second chance? Download your copy of Reckless Love now. FREE with Kindle Unlimited!

The Edge of Temptation

Chapter one
Halle

"No," I reply emphatically, hoping my tone is stronger than my disposition. "I'm not doing it. Absolutely not. Just no." I point my finger for emphasis, but I don't think the gesture is getting me anywhere. Rina just stares at me, the tip of her finger gliding along the lip of her martini glass.

"You're smiling. If you don't want to do this, then why are you smiling?"

I sigh. She's right. I am smiling. But only because it's so ridiculous. In all the years she's known me, I've never hit on a total stranger. I don't think I'd have any idea how to even do that. And honestly, I'm just not in the right frame of mind to put in the effort. "It's funny, that's all." I shrug, playing it off. It's really not funny. The word terrifying comes closer. "But my answer is still no."

"It's been, what?" Margot chimes in, her gaze flicking between Rina, Aria, and me like she's actually trying to figure this out. She's not. I know where she's going with this and it's fucking rhetorical. "A month?"

See? I told you.

"You broke up with Matt a month ago. And you can't play it off like you're all upset over it, because we know you're not."

"Who says I'm not upset?" I furrow my eyebrows, feigning incredulous, but I can't quite meet their eyes. "I was with him for two years."

But she's right. I'm not upset about Matt. I just don't have the desire to hit on some random dude at some random bar in the South End of Boston.

"Two *useless* years," Rina persists with a roll of her blue eyes before taking a sip of her appletini. She sets her glass down, leaning her small frame back in her chair as she crosses her arms over her chest and purses her lips like she's pissed off on my behalf. "The guy was a freaking asshole."

"And a criminal," Aria adds, tipping back her fancy glass and finishing off the last of her dirty martini, complete with olive. She chews on it slowly, quirking a pointed eyebrow at me. "The cock-sucker repeatedly ignored you so he could defraud people."

"All true." I can't even deny it. My ex was a black-hat hacker. And while that might sound all hot and sexy in a mysterious, dangerous way, it isn't. The piece of shit stole credit card numbers, and not only used them for himself but sold them on the dark web. He was also one of those hacktivists who got his rocks off by working with other degenerate assholes to try and bring down various companies and websites.

In my defense, I didn't know what he was up to until the FBI came into my place of work, hauled me downtown, and interviewed me for hours. I was so embarrassed, I could hardly show my face at work again. Not only that, but everyone was talking about me. Either with pity or suspicion in their eyes, like I was a criminal right along with him.

Matt had a regular job as a red-team specialist—legit hackers who are paid by companies to go in and try to penetrate their systems. I assumed all that time he spent on his computer at night was him working hard to get ahead. At least that was his perpetual excuse when challenged.

Nothing makes you feel more naïve than discovering the man you had been engaged to is actually a criminal who was stealing from people. And committing said thefts while living with you.

I looked up one of the people the FBI had mentioned in relation to Matt's criminal activities. The woman had a weird name that stuck out to me for me some reason, and when I found her, I learned she was a widow with three grandchildren, a son in the military, and was a recently retired nurse. It made me sick to my stomach. Still does when I think about it.

I told the FBI everything I knew, which was nothing. I explained that I had ended things with Matt three days prior to them arresting him. Pure coincidence. I was fed up with the monotony of our relationship. Of being engaged and never discussing or planning our wedding. Of living with someone I never saw because he was always locked away in his office, too preoccupied with his computer to pay me even an ounce of attention. But really, deep down, I knew I wasn't in love with him anymore.

I didn't even shed a tear over our breakup. In fact, I was more relieved than anything. I knew I had dodged a bullet getting out when I did.

And then the FBI showed up.

"I ended it with him. *Before* I knew he was a total and complete loser," I tack on, feeling more defensive about the situation than I care to admit. Shifting my weight on my uncomfortable wooden chair, I cross my legs at the knee and stare sightlessly out into the bar.

"And we applaud you for that," Rina says, nudging Margot and then Aria in the shoulders, forcing them to concur. "It was the absolute right thing to do. But you've been miserable and mopey and very . . ."

"Anti-men," Margot finishes for her, tossing back her lemon drop shot with disturbing exuberance. I think that's number three for her already, which means it could be a long night. Margot has yet to learn the art of moderation.

"Right." Aria nods exaggeratedly at Margot like she just hit the nail on the head, tossing her messy dark curls over her shoulders before twisting them up into something that resembles a bun. "Anti-men. I'm not saying you need to date anyone here. You don't even have to go home with them. Just let them buy you a drink. Have a normal conversation with a normal guy."

I scoff. "And you think I'll find one of those in here?" I splay my arms out wide, waving them around. All these men look like players. They're in groups with other men, smacking at each other and pointing at the various women who walk in. They're clearly rating them. And if a woman just so happens to pass by, they blatantly turn and stare at her ass.

This is a hookup bar. All dark mood lighting, annoying, trendy house music in the background and uncomfortable seating. The kind designed to have you standing all night before you take someone home. And now I understand why my very attentive friends brought me here. It's not our usual go-to place.

"It's like high school or a frat house in here. And definitely not in a good way. I bet all these guys bathed in Axe body spray, gelled up their hair and left their mother's basement to come here and find a 'chick to bang.'" I put air quotes around those words. I have zero interest in being part of that scheme.

"Well . . ." Rina's voice drifts off, scanning the room desperately. "I know I can find you someone worthy."

"Don't waste your brain function. I'm still not interested." I roll my eyes dramatically and finish off my drink, slamming the glass down on the table with a bit more force than I intend. *Oops.* Whatever. I'm extremely satisfied with my anti-men status. Because that's exactly what I am—anti-men—and I'm discovering I'm unrepentant about it. In fact, I think it's a fantastic way to be when you rack up one loser after another the way I have. Like a form of self-preservation.

I've never had a good track record. Even before Matt, I had a knack for picking the wrong guys. My high school boyfriend ended up being gay. I handed him my V-card shortly before he dropped that bomb on me, though he swore I didn't turn him gay. He promised he was like that prior to the sex. In college, I dated two guys somewhat seriously. The first one cheated on me for months before I found out, and the second one was way more into his video games than he was me. I think he also had a secret cocaine problem because he'd stay up all night gaming like a fiend. I had given up on men for a while—are you seeing a trend here?—and then in my final year of graduate school, Matt came along. Need I say more? So as far as I'm concerned, men can all go screw themselves. Because they sure as hell aren't gonna screw me!

"You can stop searching now, Rina." This is getting pathetic. "I have a vibrator. What else does a girl need?" All three pause their search to examine me and I realize I said that out loud. I blush at that, but it's true, so I just shrug a shoulder and fold my arms defiantly across my chest. "I don't need a sextervention. If anything, I need to avoid the male species like the plague they are."

They dismiss me immediately, their cause to find me a "normal" male to talk to outweighing my antagonism. And really, if it's taking this long to find someone then the pickings must really be slim here. I move to flag down the waitress to order another round when Margot points to the far corner.

"There." The tenacious little bug is gleaming like she just struck oil in her backyard. "That guy. He's freaking hot as holy sin and he's alone. He even looks sad, which means he needs a friend."

"Or he wants to be left alone to his drinking," I mumble, wishing I had another drink in my hand so I could focus on something other than my friends obsessively staring at some random creep. *Where the hell is that waitress?*

"Maybe," Aria muses thoughtfully as she observes the man across the bar, tapping her bottom lip with her finger. Her hands are covered in splotches of multicolored paint. As is her black shirt, now that I look closer. "Or maybe he's just had a crappy day. He looks so sad, Halle." She nods like it's all coming together for her as she makes frowny puppy dog eyes at me. "So very sad. Go over and see if he wants company. Cheer him up."

"You'd be doing a public service," Rina agrees. "Men that good-looking should never be sad."

I roll my eyes at that. "You think a blowjob would do it, or should I offer him crazy, kinky sex to cheer him up? I still have that domination-for-beginners playset I picked up at Angela's bache-lorette party. Hasn't even been cracked open."

Aria tilts her head like she's actually considering this. "That level of kink might scare him off for the first time. And I wouldn't give him head unless he goes down on you first."

Jesus, I'm not drunk enough for this. "Or he's a total asshole who just fucked his girlfriend's best friend," I protest, my voice rising an octave with my objection. I sit up straight, desperate to make my point clear. "Or he's about to go to prison because he hacks women into tiny bits with a machete before he eats them. Either way, I'm. Not. Interested."

"God," Margot snorts, twirling her chestnut hair as she leans back in her chair and levels me with an unimpressed gaze. "Dra-matic much? He wouldn't be out on bail if that were the case. But seriously, that's like crazy psycho shit, and that guy does not say crazy psycho. He says crave-worthy and yummy and 'I hand out orgasms like candy on Halloween.'"

"Methinks the lady doth protest too much," Aria says with a knowing smile and a wink.

She swivels her head to check him out again and licks her lips reflexively. I haven't bothered to peek yet because my back is to him and I hate that I'm curious. All three ladies are eyeing him with unfettered appreciation and obvious lust. Their tastes in men differ tremendously, which indicates this guy probably is hot. I shouldn't be tempted. I really shouldn't be. I'm asking for a world of trouble or hurt or legal fees. So why am I finding the idea of a one-nighter with a total stranger growing on me?

I've never been that girl before. But maybe they're right? Maybe a one-nighter with a random guy is just the ticket to wipe out my past of bad choices in men and make a fresh start? I don't even know if that makes sense since a one-nighter is the antithesis of a smart choice. But my libido is taking over for my brain and now I'm starting to rationalize, possibly even encourage. I need to stop this now.

"He's gay. Hot men are always gay. Or assholes. Or criminals. Or cheaters. Or just generally suck at life."

"You've had some bad luck, is all. Look at Oliver. He's good-looking, sweet, loving, and not an asshole. Or a criminal. And he likes you. You could date him."

Reaching over, I steal Rina's cocktail. She doesn't stop me or even seem to register the action. I stare at her with narrowed eyes over the rim of her glass as I slurp down about half of it in one gulp. "I'm not dating your brother, Rina. That's weird and begging for drama. You and I are best friends."

She sighs and then I sigh because I'm being a bitch and I don't mean to be. I like her brother. He is all of those things she just mentioned, minus the liking me part. But if things went bad between us, which they inherently would, it would cost me one of my most important friendships. And that's not a risk I'm willing to take. Plus, unbeknownst to Rina, Oliver is one of the biggest players in the greater Boston area.

"I'm just saying not all men are bad," Rina continues, and I shake my head. "We'll buy your drinks for a month if you go talk to this guy," she offers hastily, trying to close the deal.

Margot glances over at her with furrowed eyebrows, a bit surprised by that declaration, but she quickly comes around with an indifferent shrug. Aria smiles, liking that idea. Then again, money is not Aria's problem. "Most definitely," she agrees. "Go. Let a stranger touch your lady parts. You're waxed and shaved and looking hot. Let someone take advantage of that."

"And if he shoots me down?"

"You don't have to sleep with him," Rina reminds me. "Or even give him your real name. In fact, tell him nothing real about your-self. It could be like a sexual experiment." I shake my head in exas-peration. "We won't bother you about it again," she promises solemnly. "But he won't shoot you down. You look movie star hot tonight."

I can only roll my eyes at that. While I appreciate the sentiment from my loving and supportive friends, being shot down by a total stranger when I'm already feeling emotionally strung out might just do me in. Even if I have no interest in him. But free drinks . . .

Twisting around in my chair, I stare across the crowded bar, probing for a few seconds until I spot the man in the corner. Holy Christmas in Florida, he *is* hot. There is no mistaking that. His hair is light blond, short along the sides and just a bit longer on top. Just long enough that you could grab it and hold on tight while he kisses you. His profile speaks to his straight nose and strong, chiseled, cleanly shaven jaw. I must admit, I do enjoy a bit of stubble on my men, but he makes the lack of beard look so enticing that I don't miss the roughness. He's wearing a suit. A dark suit. More than likely expensive judging by the way it contours to his broad shoulders and the flash of gold on his wrist that I catch in the form of cufflinks.

But the thing that's giving me pause is his anguish. It's radiating off him. His beautiful face is downcast, staring sightlessly into his full glass of something amber. Maybe scotch. Maybe bourbon. It doesn't matter. That expression has purpose. Those eyes have meaning behind them and I doubt he's seeking any sort of company. In fact, I'm positive he'd have no trouble finding any if he were so inclined.

That thought alone makes me stand up without further comment. He's the perfect man to get my friends off my back. He's going to shoot me down in an instant and I won't even take it personally. Well, not too much. I can feel the girls exchanging gleeful smiles, but I figure I'll be back with them in under five minutes, so their misguided enthusiasm is inconsequential. I watch him the entire way across the bar. He doesn't sip at his drink. He just stares blankly into it. That sort of heartbreak makes my stomach churn. This miserable stranger isn't just your typical Saturday night bar dweller looking for a quick hookup.

He's drowning his sorrows.

Miserable Stranger doesn't notice my approach. He doesn't even notice me as I wedge myself in between him and the person seated beside him. And he definitely doesn't notice me as I order myself a dirty martini. I'm close enough to smell him. And damn, it's so freaking good I catch myself wanting to close my eyes and breathe in deeper. Sandalwood? Citrus? Freaking godly man? Who knows. I have no idea what to say to him. In fact, I'm half-tempted to grab

160

my drink and scurry off, but I catch Rina, Margot, and Aria watching vigilantly from across the bar with excited, encouraging smiles. There's no way I can get out of this without at least saying hello.

Especially if I want those bitches to buy me drinks for the next month.

But damn, I'm so stupidly nervous. "Hello," I start, but my voice is weak and shaky, and I have to clear it to get rid of the nervous lilt. Shit. My hands are trembling. Pathetic.

He doesn't look up. Awesome start.

I play it off, staring around the dimly lit bar and taking in all the people enjoying their Saturday night cocktails. It's busy here. Filled with the heat of the city in the summer and lust-infused air. I open my mouth to speak again, when the person seated next to my Miserable Stranger and directly behind me, gets up, shoving their chair inadvertently into my back and launching me forward. Straight into him.

I fly without restraint, practically knocking him over. Not enough to fully push him off his chair—he's too big and strong for that—but it's enough to catch his attention. I see him blink like he's coming back from some distant place. His head tilts up to mine as I right myself, just as my attention is diverted by the man who hit me with his chair.

"I'm so sorry," the man says with a note of panic in his voice, reaching out and grasping my upper arm as if to steady me. "I didn't see you there. Are you okay?"

"Yes, I'm fine." I'm beet red, I know it.

"Did I hurt you?"

Just my pride. "No. Really. I'm good. It was my fault for wedging myself in like this." The stranger who bumped me smiles warmly, before turning back to his girlfriend and leaving the scene of the crime as quickly as possible.

Adjusting my dress and schooling my features, I turn back to my Miserable Stranger, clearing my throat once more as my eyes meet his. "I'm sorry I banged into you . . ." My freaking breath catches in my lungs, making my voice trail off at the end.

Goddamn.

If I thought his profile was something, it's nothing compared to the rest of him. He blinks at me, his eyes widening fractionally as he sits back, crossing his arms over his suit-clad chest and taking me in from head to toe. He hasn't even removed his dark jacket, which seems odd. It's more than warm in here and summer outside.

He sucks in a deep breath as his eyes reach mine again. They're green. But not just any green. Full-on megawatt green. Like thick summer grass green. I can tell that even in the dim lighting of the bar, that's how vivid they are. They're without a doubt the most beautiful eyes I've ever seen.

"That's all right," he says and his thick baritone, with a hint of some sort of accent, is just as impressive as the rest of him. It wraps its way around me like a warm blanket on a cold night. Jesus, has a voice ever affected me like this? Maybe I do need to get out more if I'm reacting to a total stranger like this. "I love it when beautiful women fall all over me."

I like him instantly. Cheesy line and all.

"That happen to you a lot?"

He smirks and the way that crooked grin looks on his face has my heart rate jacking up yet another degree. "Not really. Are you okay? That was quite the tumble."

I nod. I don't want to talk about my less than graceful entrance anymore. "Would you mind if I sit down?" And he thinks about it. Actually freaking hesitates. Just perfect. This is not helping my already frail ego.

I stare at him for a beat, and just as I'm about to raise the white flag and retreat with my dignity in my feet, he swallows hard and shakes his head slowly. Is he saying no I shouldn't sit, or no he doesn't mind? Crap, I can't tell, because his expression is . . . a mess. Like a bizarre concoction of indecision and curiosity and temptation and disgust.

He must note my confusion because in a slow measured tone he clarifies with, "I guess you should probably sit so you don't fall on me again." He blinks, something catching his attention. Glancing past me for the briefest of moments, that smirk returning to his full lips. "I think your friends love the idea."

"Huh?" I sputter before my head whips over my shoulder and I catch Rina, Aria, and Margot standing, watching us with equally exuberant smiles. Margot even freaking waves. Well, that's embarrassing. Now what do I say? "Yeah . . . um." Words fail me, and I sink back into myself. "I'm sorry. I just . . . well, I recently broke up with someone, and my friends won't let me return to the table until I've re-entered the human female race and had a real conversation with a man."

God, this sounds so stupidly pathetic. Even to my own ears. And why did I just admit all of that to him? My face is easily the shade of the dress I'm wearing—and it's bright motherfucking red. He's smirking at me again, which only proves my point. I hate feeling like this. Insecure and inadequate. At least it's better than stupid and clueless. Yeah, that's what I had going on with Matt and this is not who I am. I'm typically far more self-assured.

"I'll just grab my drink and return to my friends."

I pull some cash out of my purse and drop it on the wooden bar. I pause, and he doesn't stop me. My fingers slip around the smooth, long stem of my glass. I want to get the hell out of here, but before I can slide my drink safely toward me and make my hasty, not so glamorous escape, he covers my hand with his and whispers, "No. Stay."

Want to know what happens next with Halle and Jonah? Get your copy of The Edge of Temptation now and find out. FREE with Kindle Unlimited!

Made in the USA
Middletown, DE
15 October 2020

21968552R00099